Gift

AN ENCHANTED ARDOR STORY

JODI KENDRICK

SOULGATE PUBLISHING

Dragon Island

Dragon Heat
Dragon Rogue
Dragon Blood

EveL Worlds : FUCN'A

Tough Nut
Diamond in the Ruff
Honeyed Nut
Gorilla in the Hiss
FUCN'A Collection One
Pedigree Collection

Global Paranormal Security Agency

Awakened
Surfacing
Polestar
Aquatic Investigations
Prowler

Enchanted Ardor

Gift
Wish

Finely Aged

Dragon Steel

The Kindred Chronicles

Healer
Mercenary

The Nightshade Guild

Destined Time
Trial by Blood

The Soaring Dragon Chronicles

Return Flight
Changeling

Chapter One

Olivia Boncoeur brushed the blonde bangs from her eyes as she considered the pinch-lipped woman in front of her. "You're telling me that after all these months of paper filing and follow up, that now—at this last step for approval—they've decided to withdraw their support?"

Her supervisor, Ms. E. S. Chernalog, shrugged, looking down her long nose at Olivia. "The clients have decided to invest elsewhere."

Olivia bristled, pointedly ignoring the ill feeling the woman always gave her. "This has been in the works for a very long time. Why are they backing out now?"

Ms. Chernolog glanced at her watch. "I'm no longer at liberty to discuss their portfolio. Termination papers have been drawn up. This position isn't working out and you're better employed elsewhere. I have another meeting. Janice will have your paperwork at the front desk."

"But—" Olivia gaped, chest constricting. "It's right before the Christmas holidays."

"See Janice on your way out, Ms. Boncoeur." The rigid woman's eyes flashed as she brushed past Olivia, her heels thumping on the carpeted floor on her way to the elevator.

Olivia stared after her, blinking back tears, heart twisting as her feet dragged her toward the front desk, muttering to herself, "What the frig am I going to do now? I needed this job."

"She was brought in to streamline the company and increase the bottom line, which is everything, right? I thought your work was superb. I even heard some of the execs say so." Janice scowled at Chernalog as she disappeared through the glass doors into the hall, taking Olivia's sick feeling with her.

Janice went on, gathering the freshly printed pages and manila envelope atop the desk before rummaging in her top drawer. "I was going to give you this Christmas card next week, but I guess I should deliver it now."

As an afterthought, Olivia's mind leapt to another subject of the employment topic. "Have you heard if Mr. Anderson got the security job that was open? He was desperate to find work."

"I don't hear about things like that, but Mr. Anderson did come by for an interview." Janice held up a red and gold envelope.

"Oh, that's so kind of you, Janice." Olivia dropped her security key and ID Card on the counter next to the papers, signed and slid them aside before accepting the Christmas card. She half smiled at the rounded jolly Santa head grinning at her from the front of the card as a smaller slip of paper fluttered onto the countertop.

She picked up the scroll-edged slip of beautiful calligraphic writing.

"It's a voucher for a great family-owned tea shop around the corner. I'm afraid consolation tea is all I can offer. But I find it helps."

Olivia slid her fingertip over the embossed card. "Thank you. Will you join me?"

"Too much work to wrap up since we downsized last month. You take care, and good luck with the job hunt. I'm sure you'll find something perfect for you after the holidays, but tea first." she offered a sympathetic smile. "I have a scratch ticket with my name on it at the end of the day. If I win, I'll call you for an expensive girls night out." Janice grinned.

"We need more people like you in this world," Olivia sighed, as Janice moved out from behind the counter to pull Olivia into a warm hug before she left the office for the last time.

Her thoughts and pulse resumed their race as she rode the elevator, voucher in hand.

She glanced at her watch. "May as well, since I just found an hour before I have to be at the community kitchen."

Her mind chewed over Ms. Chernalog's words.

'... you're better employed elsewhere...'

Olivia scowled, sidestepping an icy patch on the sidewalk.

Unemployed for the Christmas holidays. Fantastic predicament to be in.

She sniffled, blinking away another round of gathering tears. *It's too darn cold to cry.*

"It's okay, Liv, there's another way. There always is, so long as you keep moving forward." She nodded, her words crystallizing in the frosty air, as her breath clung to her face. "It'll have to wait till Monday, and now that I don't have any overtime workload to clear up, maybe I can call Gena over for a pajama and popcorn weekend."

Turning the corner, she strode along downtown Ottawa's lamp-lit Sparks Street Promenade, lined with nineteenth-century buildings. She pulled her coat tight against the sudden blustery squall, blowing snow down from the roofs into her face. Distracted, she almost missed the teashop, nestled between a set of arches. "How have I not noticed this place before?" Her eyes slid over the finely carved gilt sign set above the door.

'Other Worldly Teas'.

Bells jangled over the arch as she stepped into the warm shop, brushing the gritty snow from her hair and coat, stomping her feet on the mat as she looked around. Her gaze landed on a blonde woman with bright green eyes behind the counter, her smile inviting Olivia forward.

"What a lovely shop." Olivia smiled back, eyes absorbing all the beautifully restored century-old decor, as she got a sense of the place's vibe. Her fingers slid across the antique counter, fronted with windows displaying a variety of loose teas. "Is this an old grain counter?"

"It is," the woman beamed, her radiating pride soothing Olivia's worries. "I found it in an antique store down in Kingston when I had this place restored. I bought that other piece at the same time." She pointed across the shop toward another beautifully carved counter displaying packaged teas, mugs, and gifts. A framed sign nestled amid the lot advertised tea leaf readings.

I remember when counters like these were the norm in most of the shops along this street when they were built.

Olivia's gaze flowed up the carved columns supporting an intricate tin covered ceiling. "Gosh, this is just what I needed right now. I love seeing places like this treasured and preserved."

"How may I help you?" The woman's warm voice drew Olivia's attention back to the task at hand.

"Do you have a job opening?" Olivia chuckled as she held up her voucher, leaning forward to read the name tag pinned to the server's apron. "Hello, Quinn. A lovely lady sent me this way for consolation tea."

Quinn reached for the voucher, flipping it over. "Ah, yes, Janice. One of my best customers. Sorry, no employment opportunities here. I'm guessing you need something soothing?"

Olivia nodded. "I'll take whatever you recommend. I have a rather large pivot to master and no room to stumble."

"Sounds serious." Quinn glanced up from the canisters she pulled up onto the counter as she worked.

"Hmm, yes. My employment options just crumbled and I've been neglecting my savings account."

"Good time to slow down and reassess. I'm sure you'll find something suitable after the holidays." Quinn smiled handing Olivia the steaming cup. "If you'd like a reading when you're done, just let me know."

"I would love that. I have some time before I start my volunteer shift at the community kitchen up town." She brought her cup to a table by the window overlooking the pedestrian mall. Removing her coat, she settled in, extracting her notebook and pen from her purse, getting back on track while she allowed her drink to do its magic.

She made a list of priority actions.

Olivia always kept enough money in her account to cover a few months' rent. Everything else went to charities.

She sighed over the hot brew.

Tea. Job markets. New investment research.

Maybe you're just not cut out for this sort of thing, Liv. You're just not cut out for the business world.

She shivered as icy pellets skittered across the window, joining the dusting that slid along gathered snow banks, catching on the feet of huddled pedestrians.

She'd had a healthy list of options before she took this job. Now her confidence was in the basement.

This group had been her last hope and everything was set to go toward solidifying her portfolio.

How did I lose their confidence? I thought things were going so well.

And just like that—gone.

She blew on the steam, moving it across the top of the cup.

Serves me right for ignoring Bayn's suggestions of frugality and saving for rainy days.

Her old dragon shifter friend was right, though she hadn't intentionally been careless with her money. She just didn't need most of it for herself, and donated her extra earnings and time to charities, food banks and shelters. Salaries didn't stretch very far after rent, utilities, and groceries these days.

So much for the illusion of job security. I guess those days are long gone... if they ever existed.

Olivia glanced at her watch. Her heart rate accelerated, shoulders tightened, so she turned her attention back to her tea.

You've always landed on your feet.

'What we need, will come.' Abbess Marie-France used to say.

Olivia had adopted it as one of her personal mantras.

Closing her eyes, she sipped the fragrant tea, sighed and relaxed. "Perfect."

Outside the window, the promenade cleared of folks rushing home after work or streaming toward the Rideau Center for holiday shopping.

If I can't find another job, I'll have to move. Again.

Another sip.

I could reach out to Bayn... no. Too easy.

Though they hadn't seen each other in centuries, Olivia had done her best to keep tabs on him.

As much as she allowed herself to toy with the idea now and then, Olivia wouldn't ask her old friend, no matter that the dragon shifter had a treasure horde large enough to run his own country. One didn't simply ask a dragon to part with his carefully collected treasure... or old friends to solve your problems.

Olivia, you engineered this situation, you'll work your way through it.

"Reading?" Quinn made her way toward Olivia's table.

Olivia glanced at the sign. Ten dollars and the proceeds went to a local women's shelter. "Of course, how can I resist?" She checked her watch again. "But I only have a few minutes."

Quinn slid onto the seat across from her with a smile and instructed Olivia what to do with her empty cup.

"Janice said she was going to buy a scratch ticket. Should I do the same?" Olivia chuckled as Quinn peered into the cup, assessing the grounds.

"I don't know about that." Quinn squinted, turning the cup. "The leaves aren't interested in finances."

"Oh?" Olivia leaned forward, trying to peek into the cup for herself when Quinn glanced up at her with a curious eye. "What are they interested in?"

"Mostly love, but these symbols are complex. And there's a warning here. I know, that's rather vague." Quinn shrugged.

Olivia laughed as she extracted the money from her purse to place on the table. "No, that's very clear. I have zero interest in love, as it always comes with large, blaring, danger signals. Nope. Thank you. Had enough of that nonsense." She stood, re-wrapping her scarf before reaching for her coat. "I have to get going, but now that I know you're here, I'll definitely come back for more of your wonderful tea."

Quinn stood, eyes searching Olivia's face. "I'm glad to hear that, but I'd like to invite you to a party I'm hosting tomorrow night, and we can talk some more. Just give me a moment. Maybe I can help with the next step of your journey in some way." She strode toward the counter. Setting Olivia's cup and saucer aside, she reached for a business card from beside the till and scribbled on the back.

Olivia stood next to the door, buttoning her jacket, then adjusted the hood.

Quinn reached for her hand to place the card on her palm. "Please come. If you need a ride, call me and I'll arrange for someone to pick you up." She glanced out of the glass door. "And be careful out there."

Olivia's hand tingled with warmth from where Quinn's hands touched hers.

Startled, she met Quinn's green eyes and *knew* she had to go to this party, even though Saturday night was her tub and book night.

...I haven't called Gena for that movie weekend yet.

She nodded, fingers curling around the card.

Quinn smiled. "Good. See you tomorrow night."

Olivia tucked the card into her pocket and stepped out into the blustery night, pulling her hood tight to block out the howling wind and snow.

Chapter Two

Nick Klaus reached for his coffee, suppressing a sigh as he sipped the black brew. He'd lost track of the meeting's thread, somewhere in the jumble of policy and red tape.

As a representative of the council, he was obligated to attend the yearly 'State of the World' summit to decide on directions before the calendar rolled over.

Not much ever really changed. Not really.

At least I didn't have to travel to some place scorching hot this time.

The previous year's summit had been in sweltering Sydney, Australia.

Ottawa, Canada was much more comfortable.

And since he'd apparently be somewhere suitable for formal wear, his crew had decided he needed to attend a party. So, they set him up with an invitation and even a new suit.

I hate parties.

But they were serious about it, since they got him a nice one. Not red with white ermine trim like they did one year. He had checked this time, before leaving.

He sipped more of his coffee, glaring at the mediator, willing him to cut the rambling and get to the damned point.

They all knew the world was in a shitty state and that it was up to all of them to balance things through their missions.

He snorted, then drained his cup.

Nick wasn't sure it was possible. He'd been at it for over a thousand years now and not much had changed.

The speaker paused. "You disagree, Klaus?"

"People don't change. We all know this."

"It's not about us changing people. It's about us guiding them toward something better."

Nick lifted a brow. "There's a difference?"

Martin leveled his gaze on him. "Our work used to be meaningful. If we don't believe in what we do, how can we expect them to?"

"I've been telling you all for centuries, I'm not the guy for this. I'm doing it, but it isn't my calling. It was delegated to me as penance."

"Which until you find true redemption in your heart, your penance will not be fulfilled." Martin nodded.

"And I'm not a believer in the church like my predecessor was, and never will be."

"This isn't about institutions." Martin clasped his hands.

"If no one believes anymore, then this position is pointless."
Nick set his cup on the boardroom table.

"It's never pointless. Hope is all that many have." Martin
insisted.

Nick shrugged. "Find someone who believes, as you say. Let
me retire back into humanity, or do whatever comes next. If
I haven't achieved *true* redemption by now, it's not going to
happen. This isn't fair to my crew. I'm not a damned saint,
regardless of the title."

Martin spread his hands. "It's not up to me. Besides, you
signed the contract. You agreed to do the job when you saw how
many orphans you and your men left in your wake. Raids are
costly."

"Back in the days before escape clauses." Nick muttered.
"Who knew I'd be trying to atone for my crimes for so long?
And you know it was a retaliatory raid."

Martin shrugged and quickly held up a hand. "Orphans both
sides of the conflict. And yes, I know you regret that. But if
you haven't fulfilled your contract yet, then you're still missing
something, Nick. Something that Ayo set out in the terms before he passed on the mantle."

"Well, whatever the fuck it is, it's pretty damned obscure. Are
we about done here? It's the same shit every year. Unless you
have something new to tell us?"

"I have nothing more to this summit, but we are waiting for
our guest speaker to arrive from her day job." Martin glanced at
his watch. "Ms. O'Clery should be here any moment."

Several of the other attendees shifted on their seats.

"We haven't had a guest speaker in decades. This must be serious."

"Not since the great wars."

Nick sat up on his chair when a tall blonde woman with unusually bright green eyes entered the room, shaking snow from her tailored wool coat. "My apologies, I had a late customer that needed a special blend."

"Blend?" Nick lifted a brow.

"Tea." Ms. O'Clery smiled. Her gaze held his a fraction longer than one would expect of a stranger. "You're coming to my party tomorrow night."

Nick blinked. "I have an invitation to a party. I don't know who the host is."

Her grin widened in a way that Nick wasn't so sure he was comfortable with.

"Perfect. You're perfect." She mumbled, then looked to the rest of the group. "I'm Quinn O'Clery, one of the Fates."

A distinct tingle rolled up Nick's nape as the others murmured between themselves.

One of the Fates? This is new. Interesting.

But he wasn't so sure he liked how her curious gaze kept sliding back to him. And not in a 'hey you wanna hook up after this meeting' kind of eye lock.

"I won't keep you long. I'm just here to give you all a heads-up from one of my sisters." She drew a breath, choosing her words. "You may or may not be aware that we are leaning in to the

Ascension, and we're at a delicate tipping point between those driving the negative and positive forces."

Ascension?

"Like, a battle of light and dark is coming? What do you need from us? It's been a minute, but I haven't forgotten how to wield a hammer or an ax." Nick said.

Martin grunted. "We're not going into battle, Nick. That's not what we do."

"The hell it isn't. What I'm *supposed* to be doing clearly isn't doing a damned thing. I'm better suited for the battlefield. To fight for justice. Not be some shiny-eyed beacon of hope."

Ms. O'Clery turned to Nick. "My sister is working on the front lines to maintain the balance. Our job is to stay the course on the home front. It matters."

"Right. You need someone full of sunshine and rainbows to keep this up."

George turned to Nick. "Come on, Nick. In this day and age, you're the lead saint. Help the rest of us out here. Not everyone has become as jaded and cynical as you have, and we're still doing what we can to fulfill our own contracts. Some of us want to retire as much as you do, but we need to work together on this. And if what she says is true, then we need to step up."

Nick didn't respond to his colleague as a pang of guilt struck him. Everyone thought the poor guy was a giant fucking rabbit that shit out colorful eggs every year. So as much as Nick hated the cheery chubby old man persona, it wasn't so bad.

"Yeah. Yeah, okay, I'll give it some thought, buddy."

"Thank you all for your time." Ms. O'Clery smiled, reaching for her coat.

"See you next year, Nick. And good luck over the next few weeks." George said, clapping him on the shoulder.

Ms. O'Clery exchanged a few words with nearly everyone as they left, waiting until Nick approached the door.

"It's good to finally meet you, Mr. Klaus. Your friends went through a great deal of effort to ensure your party invitation. I know how busy this time of year is, but it seemed very important that you come and it's clear why, now that I've met you."

"What's that supposed to mean?"

She shrugged her slim shoulders. "You just need a little pick-me-up before the season's heavy push."

"Well it would be a little easier if the guys focused on the work to be done rather than screwing around to get me into some party."

Ms. O'Clery grinned. "Oh, this isn't just some party, Mr. Klaus. This is *my* party. And my parties aren't to be missed." She winked, pulling her coat on. "Trust me, this is just what you need. I'll see you tomorrow night."

Nick's hand tingled with warmth when she'd touched him before she disappeared through the conference room door.

He let out a long breath and growled. "I don't have time for this shit. And I don't know why you always schedule these summits during my quarter, Martin."

Martin eyed him curiously. "I've never been to a Quinn O'Clery party. You shouldn't miss it."

"Not you, too." Nick grumbled on his way out.

I really fucking hate parties.

❋

The Associate

The Associate hovered outside the conference room door, clipboard in hand, observing.

Her eyes strayed from the gathering of council members to her target—the large, blond, bearded man at the back of the room—to the snow-dusted newcomer.

It had taken a lot of effort to infiltrate her way into the organization committee just to be able to insert herself into this annual meeting, as she had done for the last decade.

Serviceable and invisible were the requirements of this role.

She rolled the disgust from her shoulders, much preferring her day job, where she held power and was the face of her company.

This required anonymity, which she would do, for the cause.

The Ascension was near and they needed to make their move.

If not this time, they'd have to wait another full year, and her employers were keen to claim this new sector before they were exposed, with everything else that had been going on.

However, this council's guest concerned her.

The Associate turned to the kitchenette, gathering glasses and water pitchers onto a tray, quickly whispering an augmentation spell bring the council's murmurs into clarity. Slipping into the conference room, she set to placing the tumblers and pitchers in place, listening.

They paused their discussion until she left. The door clicked shut and she held her breath, stationed outside the door as their conversation resumed.

Concentrating, she listened as the newcomer brought words of warning.

Fuck.

Fear and anger rippled through her.

They know. How? Doesn't matter.

Her employers will be displeased.

I will deal with this.

Message delivered, footsteps sounded before the door swung open and light conversation ensued as the council members gathered their belongings and filed past her.

Still she lingered, listening as the newcomer exchanged pleasantries.

A party.

Her target wasn't returning home right away.

Perfect.

She eased closer. The more she knew, the better.

Slipping her hand into her pocket to grasp the business cards she kept on hand, she whispered a tracking spell. She stepped forward as her target and the newcomer reached the doors, handing a card to each of them. "Thank you so much for choosing our conference facilities for your gathering. We look forward to doing business with you again."

They both accepted the cards—bearing the hotel logo and concierge contact information—with a nod as they resumed their discussion on the way to the elevator, the cards disappearing into their pockets.

The Associate smiled.

Chapter Three

Olivia checked her coat at the counter before ducking into the ladies' room to straighten her dress and make-up as the snow dusting her hair turned to a fine mist, giving it a sheen. "What are you doing here, Liv?" she muttered. "These stilettos are ridiculous and you're going to break something. You should have worn flats. Or stayed home."

At home, she'd been on the verge of calling to cancel her ride, so she could wriggle out of her dress in favor of sweatpants, when her doorbell chimed.

Discovering a fully uniformed chauffeur standing on the other side of her door, and unable to find words of protest, she bit her lip and grabbed her coat, following him to a shiny black SUV.

I can't just turn him away, he drove all the way here, from who knows-where.

After nearly an hour's drive, Olivia was second guessing her natural penchant for trusting people.

Will you never learn, Liv?

She gripped Quinn's business card on her lap, hoping she wasn't being taken to a murder house.

No. Stop that, Liv. The tea woman wasn't the type.

She didn't *feel* broken.

Gena's right, you've been bingeing too much True Crime this week.

She glanced down at the card again.

She felt... warm. And complicated.

Quinn O'Clery. Global tea purveyor and hostess.

And tea leaf reader.

Though it hadn't been much of a reading. Olivia's thoughts kept returning to Quinn's words.

Love and a warning.

Maybe she's just learning how it works? A new hobby. A warning makes sense, but love?

She snorted.

Now, she stared at herself in the mansion's powder room mirror, hands trembling. "It's fine. It's all good. Besides, you need to unwind before diving back into the job seeking slog on Monday."

She closed her eyes, drew a deep breath and left the washroom, nearly colliding with a large figure on her way past the coat check counter.

"Oh, I'm so sorry."

A large, strong hand caught her elbow as she stumbled past him, ankle tipping.

In a blink, her intuition read the power in his aura. The 'otherness' that cloaked him was similar in strength to her friend Gena's djinn, though vastly different in power. She didn't detect a beastly aspect, like the powerful dragon shifters she'd met in her time, though he was just as powerful.

It was something else.

He was something else.

Her gaze locked on his tie at eye-level, decorated with cheery little Santa heads. "Great tie."

"A gift, from guys who think they have a great sense of humor, when ties aren't optional." His voice was rich with a hint of an northern European accent that she hadn't heard since her early days wandering the continent.

She lifted her gaze to his. "Oh."

The tie was certainly at odds with the bearded face staring back at her. She registered his dark eyes first, shivering at the depths in them. There was a deep, deep, longevity in his eyes that she recognized instantly, burrowing into her. His long hair, a blend of gold, silver and platinum threads, was drawn back in thin braids from a wide forehead, with a perma-frown crease between his thick brows. Blue and black tattoos peaked out from behind the beard and crisp collar, along his muscled neck.

Her elbow remained in his firm, warm grasp.

"Well, I like it. It matches my dress," she beamed at him, though it didn't, really.

He blinked at her sudden smile, his brows descending into an actual frown as his gaze swept her classic black dress.

"I'm Olivia. Boncoeur." She held up her free hand to shake.

He immediately released her elbow, grasped her fingers and bent over them. "Nick Klaus."

"Nick Klaus—oh, I get it now. Funny friends you have."

"They think so."

She leaned in. "Don't worry, no one will ever mistake you for the real Santa Claus. You're far too trim, and certainly don't exude joviality. So, I think you're safe."

His gaze flicked over her face, full of confusion before his full lips stretched into a wide smile, exposing even white teeth as he laughed.

Deep and rich, rumbling through Liv's core in a delicious way. Her breath hitched.

"Do you have a date waiting on you?"

"Heavens, no. Last minute decision."

"Care to join me?" He lifted a brow, mischief lighting his eyes.

Olivia licked her suddenly dry lips as her heart pattered and tummy fluttered, warmth branched out through her entire body.

Oh yes, please.

She slid her fingers over his solid forearm as he led her through the cavernous foyer toward the doormen who eased massive arched doors open at their approach.

Olivia gasped. "Oh, how lovely."

Her gaze devoured the large space, decorated with luxurious precision.

"Yes, lovely." Nick's voice was low, fluttering up her nape. She glanced up to see him staring down at her.

She quickly diverted her gaze to the venue as heat bloomed in her cheeks and flushed the rest of her body.

The expanse displayed before them held a warm glow with an inviting ambiance that drew them further into the room. Candlelight flickered off gold and crystal edges, giving the space a delicate shimmer. Guests lingered at random intervals; their power signatures brushed against Olivia as they strolled past. Shifters, magic users, magic beings—some much older than herself, others not yet to their first century.

"Everything glitters, but it's all so tastefully done." Olivia breathed.

"Perfect! You're both here and you've met already." Their hostess, Quinn O'Clery, clapped her hands together as she approached them. She waved a server over, extracted two drinks from the tray, and handed them to Olivia and Nick. "So perfect. Enjoy the party."

"Already met? Didn't you want to speak to me?" Liv eyed Quinn as she rubbed her palms together, before placing a hand on each of their arms. Was there glee in her eyes? Liv turned to Nick, brow raised.

Nick shrugged.

"Damn, I'm good at this," Quinn mumbled under her breath. "No, no. Just go and enjoy yourselves. We can catch up later. Open bar. Guest rooms are upstairs."

"Guest rooms?" Liv echoed, but Quinn was already wandering toward the next arriving guests. She looked up at Nick, who surveyed the scene. "Know anyone?"

He shook his head. "Do you dance?" A layer of tension marked his brow.

"Not without breaking toes."

His brow relaxed. "I see garden doors across the room."

"An atrium? I love atriums."

"Atrium it is, then."

Drinks in hand, Nick guided Olivia in the direction he indicated, nodding here and there to other guests clustered in conversation, or couples paired off at club tables or cozy love seats.

Open Bar.

Guest rooms upstairs.

Liv bit her lip, casting glances up at Nick, struggling against the urge to lean into him.

Get a grip, Liv! You met the guy thirty seconds ago.

She sipped her drink, distantly noting it was a fine champagne.

Inhaling, she detected hints of cinnamon in Nick's cologne.

"Boncoeur. French? From Quebec?" he asked over the rim of his drink.

"I lived there for a time. Originally from France. Way back." She didn't mention that she'd sailed to New France with the Filles du Roi. "And you? Do I detect Norwegian in your accent?"

He smiled down at her, eyes crinkling in the corners. "Something like that. Way back, too."

At the threshold to the atrium, she turned into him, her curiosity uncontrollable. Glancing around at the rest of the guests, she turned her attention back to him. Heart racing, she challenged him. "Nearly everyone here is... special. With the exception of me, of course. I can sense that much. What about you?"

Liv, what is wrong with you? It's been sixty seconds, don't alienate the man before the frost even melts off your shoes!

She bit her lip again, breath held.

His gaze turned intense as he scrutinized her face, locked on her eyes, reading deep into her soul.

She couldn't breathe.

And all she should think about was kissing the full lips nestled in his soft beard and leaning into the comfort of his embrace.

She blinked, then sipped her drink again.

Jésus, Liv!

He broke into another laugh. "So much mischief in those eyes. You are as exceptional as everyone else in this place. Perhaps more so. Olivia, you are the light in the darkest winter."

Moisture blurred Liv's eyes. Her heart pounded deep in her chest as her core turned molten, melting her spine. Her breath hitched as she swallowed, licking her lips. "And you sir, are the ultimate flirt." She drank half of the remaining champagne.

He winked and tapped his nose. "And you, are a good girl." His lips curled in the corner as he finally allowed his gaze to drift below her chin.

As his gaze slid to her throat, chest and breasts, then hips down to her ankles and strappy stilettos, she forgot about the atrium and all she could think about now was that there were guest rooms somewhere upstairs.

Oh, I can be bad. So bad.

No one had ever made her feel so... desired with a *single* glance.

He met her gaze over the rim of his glass as he finally imbibed of his own drink. "Atrium?"

No.

Ninety seconds, Liv.

She nodded.

Finally turning her attention to the open room beyond the threshold, she gasped. "How enchanting!"

The atrium held the same golden glitter and glow as the rest of the manor house, but this room held a different quality to it. Magic skittered over Olivia's skin as Nick led her into the glassed-in expanse.

She felt exposed, vulnerable, as though there were no hiding secrets of any kind.

Not in this space.

And she was already prone to serious filter lapses.

This place is dangerous, Liv.

She drained her glass.

Above them, snow fell like drifting stars, melting on the glass roof in crystalline rivulets. Strings of golden beads dangled from the supports. Around them, blooms were full and heady, inviting them deeper into the creamy maze of roses, peonies, lilies and all manor of delicate flora. Candles glowed from strategic pedestals while the music from the main room lingered at the door.

The atrium stood in a hush of magic, insulated from not just the outside world, but the thriving party behind them.

Finally, she turned her attention back to Nick, who looked up through the glass roof.

The snowflakes splattered, thick and heavy against the glass. "Snowstorm?"

He nodded. "The roads will be impassable later."

"I just got here after an eternal ride with the chauffeur." She sighed, dropping her gaze to her feet. "And these shoes would not survive that much snow."

"I have a rental. I could drive you back."

"Rental? You don't live nearby, then. When do you go home?"

"Day after tomorrow. There is still a lot of work to do before Christmas Eve, though my crew are putting in a lot of extra time in my absence."

She groaned. "You're not kidding there. *So* much work to do. But that's a Monday problem." Olivia kept the bit about 'work to do' meant 'jobs to find' in her case.

"Agreed." He smiled, gaze caressing her face. "Home, or another drink?"

"Quinn did say that there are guest rooms upstairs."

"She did."

"Perhaps another drink?" She searched his face. "Unless you're anxious to go back to your hotel."

"There is no one of interest there."

Belatedly, a new thought drifted into Olivia's head. "And no Mrs. Klaus at home?"

Nick shook his head, holding her gaze. "Not at the moment."

"Well then, let's make the most of this one, enchanting night." Olivia slid her fingers along Nick's.

Subtle shocks snapped between their warm palms when he grasped her hand in his, lifting it to his lips, murmuring. "A perfect gift for the holidays."

A hundred and twenty seconds, Liv.

But she knew she was going to be in for the best snowstorm of the decade as she looked up into his face.

Maybe even a lifetime.

Chapter Four

They never did get that second drink, though they did opt for something sweet.

After an hour of hedging conversation, fingers still linked, Olivia led Nick back into the main part of the manor, mingling with other guests, then they settled on a padded velvet bench for another hour, exchanging parts of their lives in subtle drops and phrases, though they both knew neither led the mundane lives they hinted at.

She, an independent consultant and he, a mass distribution CEO.

She lifted the spoon bearing the rich pomegranate and whip cream dessert to her lips, eyes closed as she savoured the burst of flavours. Her pink tongue darted out to catch errant white fluff and Nick was nearly undone.

The mischievous sparkle in her eyes highlighted the goodness of her soul as she offered him a spoonful.

It didn't just shine in her eyes, she practically glowed with it. A spring beacon in deep winter.

Even when her expression turned sultry, her gaze devouring him when she thought he wasn't looking.

It made his chest swell every time he allowed himself to linger on her lovely face where every thought and emotion was plain for the world to see, even if she didn't give them her voice.

He accepted the offered dessert, holding her gaze as his hand slid across her thigh to her other hand resting on her lap.

So much more to her than her words described.

And despite that light and goodness, there were scars that she buried.

As they all did.

No one lived as long as they did—and Nick immediately sensed her longevity—without incurring any number of scars, shoring up their hearts.

Eventually, her glance drifted toward the ornate banister and up the stairs toward the darkened guest rooms.

A thrill of anticipation shot through Nick. He tamped it down, lest she had thoughts of sleep and nothing more.

Her gaze slid around the decorated room. The guests were thinning out, as those remaining trickled up the stairs. "Are you tired?"

She shrugged a slim shoulder, more mischief tugging at her lips. "Maybe a little. Are you?"

Nick was nearly lost in the sparkle in her eyes. "Not even a little bit, but if you'd like me to walk you to your room, I'll oblige."

"There might be hooligans up to no good lingering in the hallway." Her focus dropped to their still-entwined fingers.

He couldn't stop touching her.

Neither had seemed interested in releasing the other. The gesture held a naturalness to it that Nick had never experienced before. Not even with Hedi, his first wife. Nick shunted that memory away before it darkened the moment.

Olivia's hands belonged in his—her body linked with his in some small way.

"We can't have that." Nick agreed, his own focus landing on her soft lips.

The tip of her pink tongue slid out over her lower lip.

She eased to her feet in a fluid motion, dessert forgotten. Nick followed her up the stairs.

At the top stood a sign in a gilded frame.

'Beloved guests, please choose any room that suits you. Breakfast provided.'

"Quinn is such a thoughtful hostess." Olivia glanced up and down the hall where every door but one was closed. "There seems to only be one left."

"Then it's yours." Nick led her to it, stopped and bent over her hand, brushing his lips over the top of it. "It's been an honor, Miss Boncoeur—I never did ask if you had a mister." He straightened.

She smiled, shaking her head. "I gave up on that idea a very long time ago. I live free as a bird now."

"Now?"

Olivia shrugged. "Relationships seem to get me into more trouble than I care for. So I just avoid them now. Too much hard work and heartbreak."

"Keep your head down and focus on your work? Yeah, I can relate to that." His thumb slid over her fingers. "Good night."

He turned to go, but she hadn't relinquished his hand, tugging him back.

"Nick."

Her luminous blue gaze drew him to her.

He glanced at the crisp white bed through the open door.

Her thumb stroked along the crease of his palm, inciting a shiver through his whole body.

"There might be a hooligan lingering in there, too," she whispered.

"We can't have that either, can we?"

"I prefer not."

She crossed the threshold; Nick followed.

His gaze remained locked on her face as she scanned the room. "Looks safe enough."

"Perhaps." He leaned forward, drawn to her lovely mouth.

"You'll stay to be sure?" She mirrored him.

"How do you know *I'm* not the hooligan?"

Olivia eased the door closed behind Nick, her fingers slipped the lock. "If you are, then I want to get up to all of the shenanigans you can think of." Her free hand slid up his chest as she leaned up into him.

Nick pulled her to him, head dipping, lips descending to hers.

She was painfully warm and sweet as his insides twisted with the knowledge of her perfection.

And that smile... took his breath away.

When she finally broke the kiss, she whispered against his lips. "We have one night, Nick."

He leaned back to look down into her eyes, full of the same hope that lingered in his heart.

He nearly slid the shutter across that sentiment, as he usually did, but whatever drew him to Olivia was the same thing that stayed the closure.

Hope.

"One night." His fingers brushed the golden locks from her face, his thumb caressing her cheek and jaw. "Such a rare gift."

This, was different than any other time he'd spent a night with a woman. The same understanding, same brief exchanges, yet everything was different about it too.

So different.

There was magic in this.

It's been so long. Can I risk my heart for one night? Just one?

When he looked into her eyes, it was clear her thoughts were the same.

A risk wasn't so much of a risk, if it was just once?

They were safe with each other, this night.

Olivia finally released Nick's fingers, turning her back to him and pulled her hair aside to expose the zipper between her shoulders.

He could tell from the set of her shoulders that she held her breath.

Would he accept her offer?

How could he not?

I'm really not a saint.

Pulse ticking, Nick smiling ruefully when his fingers trembled as he reached for the button above the zipper.

Unable to resist, he pressed his lips to her nape and down her shoulder as the dress eased open, revealing her creamy back to him.

Her breath eased out on a sigh.

It was Nick's turn to stop breathing at the sight of the dark red lace. He hardened instantly.

His palms guided the fabric off her shoulders and down her arms, trailing more kisses in its wake.

She's so soft, so perfect.

Her breath hitched as goose flesh rose at his touch.

"You're cold," he murmured, hands sliding down around her midriff as the dress finally pooled at her feet.

Her response was to lean back into him, hands over his as he explored her body.

Her bottom was soft against his hard groin. She arched her back, leaving no doubt of what she wanted from him, guiding his hand across her hip and lower belly.

Her heat called to his fingers.

Resisting, Nick turned her to face him so he could reclaim her lips as he shrugged out of his jacket.

Olivia went to work on his tie, her lips opening to his, her tongue seeking and testing.

Nick made short work of the buttons on his shirt. His tie slithered to the floor, resting atop the dress as her fingers found his belt.

The heat in her eyes when she looked at him ignited a long-forgotten blaze within him.

Impatient, Olivia's hands seemed everywhere at once as Nick gave up on the clothes, needing to deepen the kiss, to possess her for as long as he had her. His hands slid up to cradle her face, focusing on her mouth, the rich flavours of the pomegranate desert still sweet on her lips and tongue.

Her hands roamed, caressing his torso and back, working their way below the band of his pants. They fell to the floor.

They both gasped when her hand closed around his hard length.

Nick broke the kiss, her name on his lips as he pressed his forehead to hers, struggling not to lose himself.

One night.

All night.

He'd make the most of it.

She'd never forget him.

He certainly wouldn't forget her. He couldn't.

Whatever magic was within her, it sought him with its delicate filigreed tendrils, testing, teasing, encircling, enticing.

He let it. For this one night.

She made him feel alive again in a way that he'd forgotten its likeness in his many long, lonely centuries.

Since he'd accepted his mission, so very long ago, shedding his mortality.

Her inner glow warmed him, crackling the unnoticed layers of stratified snow around his heart, letting them fall away for something fresh and new.

I miss this—this feeling.

Nick leaned into Olivia's grasp, one hand sliding down to pull her thigh up onto his hip. His fingers drifted along the edge of the lace bordering her panties toward her moist folds, teasing.

His head dipped down to her collarbone, lower still to taste the tops of her breasts.

"You smell amazing," he growled against her, taking control of her hands before he spilled himself right at the threshold of the door. Placing her hands on his shoulders, he pulled her other leg up, supporting her as her ankles locked behind him.

Kicking off his shoes and stepping out of the mess of clothing, Nick carried Olivia toward the bed as she held his face, claiming his lips with pure sweetness.

At the foot of the high bed, Nick lay Olivia back with the utmost gentleness, leaning over her, hip to hip, revelling in the heat of her body.

It would be so easy to slide the thin fabric aside and slip into her warmth.

Too soon.

Instead, his hands caressed her back, slipped the hooks of her bra free as he kissed and nibbled his way down her chest, taking each nipple into his mouth, sweeter than the pomegranate confection, each in its turn, fully enjoying her subtle gasps and moans.

More.

Drifting downward, his tongue circled and slid into her belly button before he pressed his face against the delicate junction of hip and thigh, kissing his way across the top edge of her panties, whispering against her heated skin. "Liv?"

"Yes," she gasped, fingers threading through his hair.

His hands slid down her hips, dragging the band down, exposing her to him.

With all gentleness, he kissed his way down her inner thigh to her knee as the scrap of fabric disappeared off the end of her foot, still clad in her strapped stilettos.

Nick's cock jerked at the sight as a barrage of images of all the ways he would have her this one night beat against his brain.

But first, he planned to worship her.

Chapter Five

Liv gasped as her gaze swept the long, hard length of the giant of a man she'd spent only hours with.

She'd thought she might find a few interesting conversations, instead, she'd monopolized the first man she met.

Now, she stared into his eyes as he gently laid her back on the high four-poster bed.

He didn't seem to mind.

And she barely noticed anyone else. As soon as she locked eyes on him, she hadn't wanted to.

Who are you, really?

You know who he is, Liv. You can feel it.

His mouth fluttered down her body, her bra disappeared.

Oh, yes, you can feel it, alright.

She hadn't missed his hardened length pressed against her nearly naked body.

Everything about him was lean and hard, covered in tattoos, and she couldn't get enough of him.

She wanted him pressed against her, filling her.

His lips lingered around her hips. He peeled her panties away, leaving only her stilettos in place.

Instinctively, her hand fell over her mound, shielding herself from his view.

He worked his way up her other leg, pressing his lips to the fingers covering her entrance.

Nick's face appeared over hers, his expression gentle, eyes searching hers.

He leaned closer, claiming her lips. She moaned, arms wrapping around his shoulders, heart pounding through her whole body.

"Ready for some shenanigans?" his low voice rumbled through her as he grasped one of her hands in his, sliding both down her belly, fingers linked, over her mound.

She smiled up into his twinkling eyes, relaxing.

The instant Liv nodded, Nick guided her fingers over her slick folds, until one of hers, and one of his, slipped into her moist heat.

She gasped as he massaged her, his hard length pressed against her thigh.

His mouth reclaimed hers until she relaxed so that her thighs parted for him.

Then he worked his way back down.

She watched him go.

She didn't resist when he moved their hands away from her entrance, or when he kissed her thigh and hooked a knee over his shoulder.

"You're so beautiful, Olivia."

Her breath hitched.

He held her gaze as his lips pressed against her nub.

"Jésus," she whispered, eyes closed, head falling back against the coverlet when his mouth locked against her, tongue swiping and suckling.

One hand gripped the bed linen, while the other needed the feel of his hair against her fingertips as he loved her with his mouth, soft beard scratching her inner thighs.

"Nick, I—," she tried to pull away as the pressure inside her mounted.

His arm locked around her hips, holding her in place as he devoured her passion, as he forced her to crest the dam holding everything that she was back.

Body coiled, every worry rose to the surface. With a deeply held gasp, she let it all go.

Eyes closed, her world went as white as the chaotic snow-storm beating at the windows beyond the heated shelter of their cozy room.

Dimly, Liv was aware that he kissed his way back up her body, joining her on the mattress and gathered her limp form into his arms like an over-sized rag doll, warming her back with his broad chest and thick arms.

He was still hard, and pulsing against her bottom, though he made no move to take her.

He tipped her chin toward him, claiming her mouth as she caught her breath.

Still he didn't take her.

Her hand slipped behind her, travelling down his muscled body until she could wrap her fingers around his silky hot length, stroking, encouraging, as her ardor built anew.

Liv rubbed her bottom against him so that he slid between her thighs.

He groaned her name. "Who is the hooligan now?"

"You're the shenanigan instigator. I'm just following through."

He chuckled against her mouth.

Her thighs clenched around him, eliciting a gasp.

She tilted her hips so that his tip aligned with her entrance and waited.

Still he didn't move.

He pulsed against her. Her insides throbbed with need.

His lips drifted along the shell of her ear and down her throat, his hands working her breasts, fingers on her sensitive nipples.

"Nick," she breathed.

He reclaimed her mouth, his fingers drifted down to splay across her lower belly.

Finally when she couldn't stand it anymore, with his strong hand holding her securely in place, he thrust forward, striking her sensitive sweet spot, filling her with perfection.

She cried out, inner muscles clenching him in place, secured against his lap.

Slow and steady, he ground up into her and out just enough to allow every inch behind the head to slide along her channel.

One night.

The building haze enveloped her when she suddenly needed to see him. To look into his eyes.

Wriggling free, she linked her fingers with his and disengaged so she could turn around. Claiming his mouth, her breasts dangled, nipples scraping along the hair on his chest as she straddled him.

Sitting up, his arms encircled her waist, dragging her down atop him, locking her into place again, mouth closing on one nipple, then the other.

"Nick," she gasped, unable to stop herself as the sensation of his tongue, silky and firm, ignited her need to grind faster.

"Olivia."

His low voice calmed the rising urgency. She drew a deep breath, hands cradling his face so that she could focus on his mouth, tongue dancing with his as she brought her hips under control, prolonging the moments.

One night. All night.

Her heart twisted.

Opening her eyes to his depths, so open, so clear, so beautiful—she knew.

A heart shadowed with pain and loss, but ultimately true.

She would never, ever forget this night.

It would remain one of her most cherished memories, for however much longer she decided to live, unless snuffed from this world forcefully.

No regrets.

She closed her eyes, blocking out the vision of his soul that brought an ache to her heart.

No, that wasn't right. There would be one regret. The one that meant she'd never see him again after this night.

He'd go back to whatever his life held for him, and she'd return to her busy life and quiet bed.

His gentle fingers pushed her hair back from her face, drawing her attention back to his.

She sensed the subtle resistance in him as he held back.

Olivia didn't want him to hold back, she wanted all of him the way he'd had all of her.

Holding his dark gaze, she observed the subtle signs as she moved her hips, tightening and releasing.

Nick closed his eyes, leaning his forehead against her chest, tilting his hips away from her. "Olivia."

She locked herself around him, thwarting his escape.

"Liv," his breath shook.

None of the lovers or partners she'd taken over the years had ever incited the perplexing depth of emotion that she felt now as she held his gaze.

He frowned, the laugh lines around his eyes tightened as he resisted the climb.

She worked him, mercilessly, desperate for this ultimate give and take.

His breath shortened, jaw clenched.

She sensed how close he was despite his resistance, spiking her own ardor.

She watched all the subtle signs, allowing her own need to rise, matching his, as he'd done for her—until she'd taken control.

Her heart pounded in her chest, pulse ticked in her ears.

Nick's entire body went taught with warning. "Liv."

"Yes, Nick," she whispered by his ear, her channel walls clenching harder.

He groaned, arms crushing her to him as he buried his face in her chest, his breath hot between her breasts.

The sensation of him swelling inside her tight sheath sent her over alongside him, slick bodies clinging, lest she spiral off the edge of the world.

Their spent breaths filled the sudden silence of the room as their heated limbs cooled around each other, still joined.

Nick placed the gentlest of kisses on Olivia's heart before looking up into her eyes, whispering "Perfection."

He reached down behind her, fingers slipping the straps of her stilettos, freeing her feet before he rolled her under the bed linens, cocooning them.

He continued to kiss and explore her body, so full of worshipful gentleness that it made Olivia's heart ache with it.

Never in her long life had anyone been so tender as this large, bearish man and their one night together.

No regrets, Liv.

Chapter Six

Nick followed Liv, fingers entwined, down to the breakfast hall where other couples from the party lingered.

Neither of them mentioned the inevitable parting, but their constant need for some small contact spoke volumes.

His eyes strayed to her face again and again, often meeting her gaze as she sought him out in return.

I can't let her go... but I can't keep her either.

There was no room in Nick's world for a love he knew she would offer, should she want him in return.

That kind of magic wasn't meant for him.

Their night together was all that he could have.

"As soon as the roads are clear enough, I can drive you home."

Her blue eyes lifted from her plate, over their small table, searching his face. "If it isn't out of your way, I'd like that."

He nodded.

Nick had no idea where she lived in relation to his hotel, but didn't care, he'd drive as far as he needed to see her home safe. And to greedily take all the extra time he could steal, before he had to let her go.

Eyes fixed on her plate, her fork poked at the fruit. "Your flight is early tomorrow?"

"Very."

She nodded.

Breakfast finished, they made their way to collect their coats, where Quinn met them with sparkling eyes, handing each of them a card. To Olivia she said, "A few downtown businesses to consider. Tell them I referred you. Just...remember your reading."

Turning to Nick, she held his gaze a long moment as she considered her words. "Please... remember to stay the course."

Reaching out she took each of their hands, drawing a deep breath. "I have so much hope for each of you." She squeezed their hands and released them. "Safe drive home."

"Thank you for the wonderful evening, Quinn," Olivia smiled back at their hostess.

Nick led Olivia down the broad front step to where a valet had delivered his rental, cleared of snow and ready to go.

Olivia's attention turned away from the vehicle, frowning at a figure lingering in the shadows at the edge of the building, too far to observe detail beyond the nondescript sense of the staff uniforms. Nick reached to open the door for her to get in before rounding to the driver's side. "Is something wrong?"

She turned her gaze to his eyes, her expression cleared, replaced with a brilliant smile. "Everything is just perfect."

As soon as they were on the road, Nick noted Olivia's attention drifting toward the passing scenery, Quinn's card flipping over and over in her hands, and murmured, "That was... cryptic. 'Remember your reading'?"

"Hmm? Quinn O'Clery? Yes, a unique woman." She smiled at Nick. "She read my tea leaves the other day. 'Love and a warning', she'd said, then invited me to her party. I think maybe she still needs a little practice with her predictions." Her gaze turned inquisitive. "Stay the course, huh?"

Love?

Nick lifted a brow.

Quinn had said that she was one of the Fates. That tingling sensation worked its way up Nick's nape again.

What is she up to?

"Yeah, reference to my work."

Olivia turned her full gaze to his profile as he drove. "You're thinking of changing careers?"

"Retirement would be nice."

Retirement.

Nick dismissed the mixed feelings that specific word brought.

She laughed, eyes trained on his face, assessing. "Surely you're not old enough for that." Her bright eyes swept his features. "No, wait, never mind. I'm forgetting myself. I know better than to be so quick to judge something like that."

Nick laughed then, as he recalled her comment the previous night about the special status of the other guests. "Look at us still keeping our secrets close to the vest."

"Who says I have secrets?" Olivia challenged him. "I'm an open book."

"Me too."

She snorted and laughed. "You're anything but."

He glanced her way. Her eyes shone with challenge.

"An exchange then. You go first. I know you've been around much longer than you look."

She nodded considering this. "As have you."

"I have."

"How long?" She lifted a perfect blond brow.

"Longer than you. What are you? Two, three hundred?" He threw the numbers out there, expecting less than half that. "You don't look a day over twenty-five."

"Not bad. Five and a half centuries, thereabouts. I lost track after midlife."

Nick laughed. "No kidding? But *not* a shifter? I thought I detected a subtle hint of dragon signature on you."

"Funny, I'd have asked the same of you, though I didn't think that was right either."

"So, you *do* know some dragons?"

Olivia shrugged. "Maybe one or two may have rubbed off on me somewhere along the way."

"Intriguing, you'll have to tell me about that some day."

Her expression turned solemn, her voice soft. "Some day." Her attention flicked back to the window.

One night.

Nick sighed.

"My longevity was the gift of a djinn, a long, long time ago. And yes, it involved a dragon." She turned her direct gaze back to his profile.

He met her eyes.

The truth in her words knocked around in his chest.

Intriguing.

Now he really wanted to hear that story.

"Your turn."

"Former warrior. A little too much raiding. Gave up my weapons for a magic bag."

It was her turn to lift a brow, waiting for more.

He pointed at his chest, fingertip landing on the silk tie his crew had given him.

Olivia's wide eyes dropped to the cheery Santa heads. "You're not freaking serious."

"I am."

In seconds, her expression altered several times, from delighted shock, confusion to concern. "But you want to retire and Quinn wants you to 'stay the course'?"

"She does."

"Who would replace you?" Her voice went up.

"No idea."

"But, you don't want to do it anymore?"

"Never really did."

"Then…how?"

"Atonement."

A soft "Oh."

"Yeah."

"So you don't believe." She swallowed. "You don't believe in the work that you do?"

"I know it has a purpose. I'm just not the true guy for the job. Not my calling."

His gut twisted when he caught the sadness in her expression, and he couldn't help feeling like he'd just let her down somehow.

"It's just—so important."

The twist wrenched a little deeper. Nick rolled away the discomfort creeping into his shoulders.

This was a bad idea.

Their perfect night was being tainted by the reality of daylight.

Silence fell between them until they reached the city limit and she had to guide him to her neighborhood with muted directions.

He pulled up in front of her building.

She reached for the door handle, pausing. "Thank you for last night, Nick." Her blue gaze met his. "It was… special. And for the ride. I hope it's not too far out of your way." She rushed through the last words.

Nick's hand shot out to grasp her left hand before she opened the door, staying her movement.

I shouldn't touch her anymore...

She looked down at their hands, his fingers caressing hers. "Yes, it was special, Olivia. *You're* special."

He met her blue gaze. Her pale cheeks flushed as she dropped her gaze back to their hands.

He didn't tell her that his hotel was only a few blocks away. It didn't matter.

It was just one night.

They wouldn't see each other again.

Pain shot through his heart as he searched her solemn face, still turned downward to their hands.

His thumb eased over the backs of her fingers, reluctant to let her go just yet. Or ever.

When she finally lifted her gaze to his, her blue eyes were clear and determined. "If you're serious about moving on, I would do it."

"Do what?"

"The job."

He blinked, heart flipping through several beats. "You would replace me?"

She nodded. "If you no longer wish to do it, and there is no one else. I would... do it. Whatever that means."

He squeezed her fingers, a smile touched his lips. "That's kind of you."

She glanced out of the window up at her building. "You know where I live now. Give it some thought, though I imagine there'd be a lot of training involved."

Nick didn't laugh.

She was serious.

He lifted her fingers, pressing his lips to them one last time before he released her. "I will certainly give you thought."

She nodded, left the vehicle and dashed in through the front doors of her building, her red stilettos dancing over clumps of wet snow and icy puddles.

He stared after her, long after the glass doors drifted closed.

A car horn honked, urging him to give up his space in front of the building. Throwing the SUV into gear, he navigated to his hotel, lost in thought.

Chapter Seven

"My goodness, Olivia, what the heck were you thinking?" Olivia stared at her reflection in the steamy bathroom mirror. Her lips were still love-swollen and her body hummed from her magical night with Nick.

One night.

Maybe he wasn't truly serious.

Maybe he wasn't really the fabled St. Nick at all. He'd just said that to give her... something.

But what if it's true?

He'd seemed so... solemn when she'd first bumped into him. Sensed the deep sadness.

Sensed the longevity, and the levity that it brought to someone that was long lived.

Olivia had seen it before, though she'd been resistant to it herself.

Because she staved it off with her constant busyness. Her missions and crusades to help others—to fill her time and give herself purpose.

Meaning.

Give herself a reason to be on the planet. To make the most of the gift she'd been given.

It wasn't that she didn't ever feel the weight of it.

And perhaps that was what fueled her determination.

She'd always had the choice. Even now.

Nick didn't? Hadn't he ever?

Surely he had.

What had he said?

'Atonement'.

A choice born out of guilt.

Not a calling, as he'd said.

"It doesn't matter." She swiped at the fog on the mirror, brushing her wet hair.

There was a lot of work to do, especially now that she had to look for a new job.

Last night had been beautiful. Magical. Some one else's world.

A fantasy.

Today, she was firmly back in the real world.

She moved into her bedroom, ignoring the party dress strewn across the bed, red shoes abandoned at the foot, her lacy bra and panties a bundled heap next to them.

Heat infused her face as memories of Nick surged back into her mind, hot and vivid.

Her fingertips drifted across her sensitive lips.

She shivered with the recollection of his touch, his lips on hers, the sensation of his large hands on her body. The heated look in his eyes as he carried her to the bed, then when he relieved her of those particular lacy bits.

The press and weight of his body.

The pleasure he'd brought her.

He'd gifted her with a night of lovemaking like she'd never experienced in her long life.

No lover had ever been so generous and attentive to the needs she didn't know she had.

I guess I just always picked the wrong men...

One night.

Now a precious memory.

She drew a shaking breath, grasped the clothing and stuffed it all in the hamper. The shoes hit the back corner of her closet, evicting the incessant replays from her mind.

Now, Liv.

Today.

Focus on today, not a dream world.

Standing in the middle of her room, towel wrapped around her damp body, she searched for something to anchor herself.

Quinn's white card gleamed from her dresser top.

Yes.

Employers to contact.

Work to do.

Rent and bills to pay.

A steady breath.

She pulled on her jeans and a knit shirt before going in search of a light lunch.

There was much work to do. There always was.

Nick surveyed his empty hotel room.

Before last night, it was just a room. Somewhere to sleep while not at home.

Now, its emptiness loomed. Mocked him for the decades—centuries—that he'd been alone. Since Hedi.

It wasn't as though he hadn't had time to grieve. He had.

But now, he was locked into what seemed to be an eternity of aloneness.

Removing his coat and boots, he set them aside along with thoughts of the past, memories so distant they deserved to be laid to rest.

Should be laid to rest.

Hedi would have wished it. Would have been pleased to see him find some joy in another after so long.

He stripped, laying his suit over the desk chair, shoes placed below it.

Lack of sleep dragged at him while his body still crackled with memories of Olivia.

Her bright blue eyes, the parting of her full lips in smile. Her gentle moans and sighs as he made love to her.

His body responded.

He cranked the shower lever to blast himself with cold water, hoping to cool the rush.

Her presence had made him feel more alive than he had in centuries. Not since his days rooted in humanity.

Though not nearly as old as he, she had some understanding of what it was like to be around longer than most.

How did she do it?

Keep that bright, hopeful quality that she glowed with?

Nick scrubbed his face under the cold water, seeking relief from the love buzz he couldn't shake, while his heart weighed heavy with her words during their long ride back to the city.

'You don't believe in the work that you do?'

The sadness in Olivia's voice and her eyes as she studied him.

Her need to believe.

The heart of a crusader.

Was that what drew him to her?

The need to make things right?

That light in her that fueled belief in doing what was right simply because it was important?

Maybe that's what was wrong with Nick. It was a necessary job, but he'd never believed what he did was important. That it mattered.

Why should it?

Hedi would have called it 'duty'.

It seemed so pointless to spend year after year carefully cultivating the groves for one brief period of pollination.

For centuries.

The world didn't seem to be any better off than when he'd started.

I've failed.

I've been failing the world for centuries and just didn't care enough to examine that.

Olivia's voice full of conviction floated back to him.

'...I would do it.'

Nick chuckled.

Now *she* was the kind of soul the council needed to push the changes they'd been striving for.

Real changes.

The kind of champion that could lead the world toward the bright side.

Unless the reality of the world eventually *could* weigh on her, as it had Nick.

Leaving her just as apathetic and weary.

No.

Not Liv.

She still burned bright, despite five centuries on this planet.

Ayo should have handed her the mantle, not me.

Timing?

Maybe he would have, had she been born under the right arc of stars.

Instead, he'd found me, covered in grime and heartache, and nearing my last breath...

Nick dried and dressed, pulling on jeans and a long sleeve t-shirt. He still had a bunch of hours to kill, and energy to spend before his time began to wane; he might as well explore the city.

He laced his boots and grabbed his leather jacket with the thermal liner. He didn't mind the cold, but wasn't impervious to it, and Ottawa in December was frigid. Exhilaratingly so.

He explored the Rideau Centre, walked along the freezing canal, admired Chateau Laurier and toured the Parliament buildings.

It was dark by the time he wandered back along the Sparks Street Promenade, where a quaint tea shop caught his attention.

Through the glass window, he saw a blond woman organizing tea tins along the back wall.

Quinn O'Clery?

Curious, he mounted the steps and pushed the door open.

She glanced up as winter air blustered inside along with him.

She smiled. "Hello, Nick. Tea?"

He nodded. "May as well." He stomped the snow from his boots on the mat before striding deeper into the shop, as his gaze swept the interior. He smiled at the framed sign for readings. "You going to read me too?"

Quinn's gaze flicked to the sign, her lips stretched with a grin. "Of course."

"Liv thinks your reading is off the mark. That you're new at this."

Quinn lifted a blond brow as she prepared Nick's tea. "I'm never off the mark."

"As one of the Fates, I should think not." He picked up various items off the counter, inspecting them as she worked. "Though vague. 'Love and a warning'?"

"Vague? Seems specific to me."

"Well I'm not interested in her love life. But I am concerned about this warning."

Quinn's other brow rose as a smile tugged at her lips. "You're not, huh?"

"Is she in danger? Or just a matter of bad luck in business kind of warning?"

"Both."

Nick's heart thumped. "Well that kind of message needs some specifics, don't you think?"

"I can't interfere."

"The hell you can't. If you can give warnings, you can be more specific."

Quinn shook her head. "I can't influence the circumstances."

"You invited her to your party for a reason." Nick's gaze shot to Quinn's face, eyes narrowing on her delicate features. "So that we could meet? Why?"

She shrugged a slim shoulder.

"Isn't that meddling?"

"There are rules, Nick. You have rules. I have rules too." She poured hot water into the cup and slid the saucer toward him.

"Besides, your invitation was by request. If you're looking for meddlers, turn your attention to your buddies back home."

"Your appearance at our council meeting defies that statement."

"That was a message from my sister. A favor to her. Not my lane." She glanced at the clock on the wall. "Drink up, I'm closing soon."

Nick lifted a brow. "Got more important things to do?"

"No, but you do."

Nick grunted and sipped the hot, aromatic brew. "Not bad."

Quinn's lips quirked as she stowed the tins she'd used to make his tea.

When he finished, he slid the cup and saucer across the counter.

She picked it up with perfectly manicured fingers, turning the delicate porcelain cup between them.

She frowned.

"What is it?" Nick leaned over the counter to peer into his cup. It just looked like a mess of tea dregs.

"Looks like a blizzard in there. Change. You're in for a lot of change and you have some big decisions to make."

"Change? Nothing ever changes. And what do you mean by 'big decisions'?"

Quinn shrugged. "Closing time. You have to go." She glanced at the clock again. "Now."

Nick blinked, taken aback. "Thanks for the tea." He pulled out his wallet.

Quinn waved his money away. "On the house. Take care and remember to stay the course, Nick. It's important." She came around the counter, ushering him toward the door. "I suggest going left."

Nick was barely down the steps when she threw the lock and killed the lights. He stared at her through the window.

She tilted her head to her left and waved.

Adjusting his jacket, Nick nodded and strode in the suggested direction, trying to make sense of the encounter, muttering. "Strange woman."

The promenade was blocked with construction barriers, so he turned again, lost in thought.

What did any of it mean?

Quinn is a Fate, it has to mean something. But what?

Liv's warning returned to his mind. Danger.

Did she know that? She hadn't seemed to take it seriously, but he doubted she knew Quinn was a Fate and that her messages had weight.

She needs to know.

Nick glanced up at the surrounding office buildings, set on finding his way back to her condo.

Snowbanks piled up on sidewalks made them impassable, and diverting his attempts to head in the right direction. Instead, he found himself on a darkened stretch near an old church.

Several rough sleepers headed up the front steps, engaged in their conversation, ignoring Nick as he bypassed them.

"I wonder what the soup is tonight."

"Who cares? It's always good when Miss Olivia hands it to you."

"True. Hey, do you think she's one of us?"

"Who knows? She does seem to understand us better than anyone else ever has and.."

Pausing, Nick's attention followed them as they disappeared into the church.

Were they talking about *his* Olivia?

Certainly sounded like it.

A woman's voice echoed up from the alley just beyond the edge of the building. "I already told you I can't help you, Mr. Anderson. Now please go home, it's cold out and there are many folks inside that need their hot meal."

Nick edged closer, peering around the corner. Olivia stood in the alley without her jacket, trash bag in hand.

The temperature had dropped considerably and quickly became bitter.

"You said your company was going to hire me and I told you how important this is to me. I have to support my kid."

"I said I was hoping that they would seriously consider you. And as I've already explained, I have no control over who they take on. I thought they hired you already."

"And I told you I needs this." Anderson snarled as he pushed Olivia up against the wall.

The trash bag hit the ground as she cried out with his arm pressed across her throat.

Nick tensed, stepping into the alley.

She shoved him away. "I can't change anything. Go home."

"Bitch! I won't let you patronize me like that!" Anderson's left fist swung out. Light glinted off metal as his right hand arced down toward Olivia. "She said you were scamming everyone, laughing at us while living it up. I saw you—all fancy and—she said you were playing around with us. That you don't care about—,"

Liv's hands came up to block the coming blow.

"No!" Nick's hand shot out, freezing both of them.

Chapter Eight

Nick ran forward, grabbed Anderson by the back of his jacket and threw him backwards against the opposite wall. The knife clattered to the ground as he unfroze with a groan.

"What—what just happened?" Olivia panted, wide eyes on Nick. "Where did you come from?"

"I was just coming to—Quinn said..." Nick's gaze dropped to the man staggering to his feet.

Nick rounded on him, grabbing him by the front of his jacket, slamming him up against the brick wall so that his feet dangled above the snowy ground. "What the hell is wrong with you, pulling a knife on her?" He snarled into the man's terrified face, slamming him a second time so that his head cracked backward.

His head lolled.

"Nick, please don't hurt him. I'll call the police." Olivia pulled the back door open.

Nick let him drop to the ground unconscious, with a grunt of disgust.

"Molly call Graham. Mr. Anderson needs a ride home." Olivia called in through the open door.

"I thought you said you were calling the police?"

"Graham is the local constable that patrols this area. He knows everyone in this district."

"And you're just going to send him home? He should be charged and arrested."

"And his daughter will have no one to support her." Olivia rounded on Nick.

"Olivia, he had a knife and was about to stab you. He would have killed you."

Her eyes flicked to Anderson's inert form as she straightened, drawing a deep breath.

Tires crunched over ice and snow as a black and white cruiser pulled up at the end of the alley.

"Liv?" The constable called as he got out of the vehicle, approaching the alley, his gaze swiveling from Olivia to Nick to the unconscious man on the ground and back to Nick. "Is there a problem here?"

Liv waved a hand toward her attacker. "Mr. Anderson needs a ride home."

"Mr. Anderson needs to be charged with attempted murder," Nick spat. "He tried to stab you, Olivia."

"But he didn't."

"Thanks to your friend here?" The constable nodded toward Nick as he straightened from inspecting Anderson.

"Nicholas Klaus," Nick said.

"Constable Graham Greer." He held out a hand to shake.

Surprised, Nick accepted it.

"Liv, you've got to be more careful. Mr. Klaus is right, you should press charges."

"I'm sure I would have been fine."

The constable lifted a brow. "One of these days Liv, your luck is going to run out. Your heart is bigger than your common sense, some times."

Olivia bristled. "He needs help and so does his daughter. I stepped out with a trash bag and everything happened so fast." She turned her attention to Nick, studying him again.

"My point exactly," Graham said. "I'll take Anderson to the hospital to be checked out. He may have a concussion. Do you know why he attacked you?"

"He apparently didn't get the job I recommended him for, again. He's desperate to keep his teenage daughter, and he can't do that without a job."

Nick poked at Anderson's knife with his boot, drawing the constable's attention to it. "When he swung at you, he said 'She said you were playing around'. Do you know what that meant? Who is 'she'?"

Olivia shrugged. "No idea. But I never would do that."

"I know you wouldn't, Liv." The constable picked up the knife with a gloved hand and dropped it into an evidence bag. "I know you keep trying to help him. Everyone knows."

"I-I told him there were no guarantees." She turned sad eyes to the unconscious man. "He's persistent, but he's never been violent before. I'm not sure what prompted this."

Constable Greer nodded. "It's freezing out here, you should grab your jacket and I'll give you a lift home."

Liv shook her head. "I still have dinner to serve here."

Graham shook his head. "So stubborn."

"I'll stay and walk her home when she's done." Nick said to the constable. "I'll help you get this guy into your cruiser."

Nick lifted the wiry man from the ground, trying not to inhale too deeply of the rancid body odor that enveloped him with a hint of overlaying sulfur.

"Graham, you'll ask him what he meant? Who he was speaking about?" Olivia followed them to the cruiser.

Several shelter patrons lingered on the front step watching.

"Of course." The constable said to Olivia as he studied Nick maneuvering the full grown man with ease. He held Olivia's gaze, his eyes flicking to Nick and back. "You'll be okay here?"

She put a hand on Graham's arm with a nod before he got into the cruiser.

Nick put an arm around her and she leaned into him for his warmth as they watched the vehicle pull away.

"You okay, Miss Olivia?" One of the patrons called from the front door.

"All good. Go on inside, Mr. Lacroix." She called back. Lowering her voice, she turned to Nick. "Thanks for that. I'm not sure how you did that, but I'm grateful for your help. You don't need to stay."

"I'll walk you home. Need an extra set of hands?"

Olivia's brows went up as she looked into his face. "I've been walking myself home my entire life, Nick. But we can always put an extra set of hands to work here." She slid her hand into his, leading him back down the alley, letting go only long enough to finish putting the trash bag into the bin, which Nick did before she could reach it.

Following her inside, they washed up and got to work.

"The apron suits you," Olivia grinned as he tied the strings behind his waist, studying the trays of thick pea soup, dinner rolls and pudding.

Nick maintained his position alongside Olivia and the other staff working the meal shift, serving the vulnerable, observing how she interacted with the diners and their regard for her.

When Nick ventured into the back for more coffee, an old man, gruff and worn, with a milky left eye, sighed as she handed him a tray of food.

"Don't like pea soup, Mr. Ayotte?" Olivia asked, pouring a cup of tea for him.

"Not particularly." He accepted the hot tea with a nod.

"Lasagna tomorrow night."

Mr. Ayotte smiled with an exaggerated wink with is good eye. "My favorite. This'll do until then."

Olivia beamed at him. "Enjoy."

The old man turned away, shuffling along before Nick returned.

"You've been doing this a long time." Nick set a rack of clean mugs on the counter, then placed another loaded bowl onto the next empty tray.

"You could say that." Olivia smiled as she handed off the prepared meal. "Seems like you have some experience serving crowds too."

He shrugged, filling the next bowl. "Why do you do it?"

"It's needed. And so long as organizations like this are needed, I will do what I can to help. Everyone needs a friendly face and a little lift to their day." She shrugged. "The world is an unkind place."

"And you've experienced your fair share of it."

"I have—be careful Mrs. Hopkins, the soup is very hot. Miss Molly will be around with your pudding in a few moments, she needed to get more from the back."

Mrs. Hopkins smiled, toothless. "Just what I need." Her watery eyes slid up to Nick. "New friend?"

"Indeed. This is Mr. Klaus. He's visiting the city for the weekend and was kind enough to lend a hand tonight."

Mrs. Hopkins' eyes crinkled. "You ladies are all lovely, but it's so nice to see a handsome face now and then."

Nick chuckled bowing to Mrs. Hopkins. "I needed to see the very best residents of the city."

"Oh, such a flirt! Don't lose sight of this one, Miss Olivia." Ruddy cheeks deepening, Mrs. Hopkins giggled.

"I shall do my best, now rest and enjoy your meal."

Eventually the diners thinned out as they made their way to bed down for the night. Nick helped Olivia and the staff clear away the empty dishes and put away the tables and chairs.

The last of the staff left the two to lock up. When Olivia lifted the next trash bag to be discarded, Nick quickly took it from her and put it in the dumpster himself, returning to wash his hands.

Olivia shook her head, chuckling as he re-entered. "Thanks, but I doubt anyone else will be lurking out there again."

"Never know." Nick shrugged, reaching for their jackets, pulling Liv's over her shoulders. He stared down into her up-turned face, thoughts returning to their banter about hooligans the previous night, unable to resist her soft lips. He pulled her jacket closer and bent to press his lips to hers. "I'm going to miss you, Olivia."

He leaned his forehead against hers, reveling in the nearness of her.

"Me too, Nick." She leaned back, looking up into his face and smiled. "You can visit any time. As I said, we always have need of extra hands." Her smile turned mischievous, eyes twinkling.

Nick shook his head, releasing her, but allowed his hands to drift down her shoulders and arms, not quite ready to let go completely just yet. "I don't know how you do it. Keep your spirit so high... after everything."

"Survival skill." She lifted a shoulder, then turned her attention to the buttons on her coat. "Just as I suspect your grumpiness usually keeps people at a distance. Usually." When she looked up at him again, her eyes shone even brighter. "But I'm a grump magnet. It is my mission in life to clear away the thunder clouds and let the sunshine burn away the negativity fog."

"Is that a challenge?" Nick opened the door for her and waited on the step as she locked it.

Slipping the keys into her pocket, she turned to him. "Absolutely. But that will require regular contact. Say, at least once a year? How about we turn our meeting to an annual dinner date?"

Nick's heart tripped at the thought of seeing Olivia again and on a regular basis. But part of him balked at the notion of going a whole year in between each visit.

That wouldn't do.

"Perhaps. We can discuss the details and requirements of this challenge on our way back to your place." He held out a gentlemanly hand for her to precede him to the sidewalk from the alley.

She glanced around the shadowy alley, surreptitious, shivering. Instead of leading, she took his hand, walking side by side toward the road. "Of course."

Nick swallowed at the flicker of fear in her eyes before she cleared it away.

He pulled her close, tucking her against his side, arm around her.

She snuggled in as they strolled along the darkened street, streetlamps illuminating the snow swirling around their feet.

"Wherever we meet must have an atrium."

"Agreed." He glanced down at her face obscured by her hair drifting on the frigid eddies.

The tip of her nose had turned pink from the cold. "And a nearby guest room?"

Nick's chest thumped. "Absolutely."

Olivia suddenly stiffened against him, her head turning, eyes squinting into the darkness across the road.

"What is it?"

"I—I think we're being followed."

Chapter Nine

Olivia shivered against Nick's warm side, attempting to keep the conversation light.

The moment they reached the end of the alley next to the church, apprehension slithered up her nape.

You're just unsettled from Mr. Anderson's visit earlier. You're fine, Olivia.

Quinn's tea warning is getting to you.

Still, she scanned the darkness as she led Nick toward her building, taking comfort in his presence, negotiating their light-hearted annual challenge.

How had he done it? Had he somehow frozen time to stop the attack?

She'd been chewing it over all evening, desperate yet reluctant to bring it up.

She looked up into his solemn face. Ice crystallized his brows and beard, giving him an otherworldly appearance as they passed under the streetlamps.

Compartmentalize, Liv. Put it away and focus on the here and now. He's leaving tonight.

Her chest tightened.

But I will see him again next year. Maybe?

She clung to that win.

Movement drew her attention to the shadows across the narrow street. An obscure shadow slid from dark patch to dark patch, matching their pace.

"I—I think we're being followed."

At the next lamp, Nick turned her so that her back was to the street, adjusting her collar.

He drew a deep breath, paused and dipped his head to kiss her, whispering. "I can't see anything, but I feel something nearby."

"In the shadows," she breathed against his mouth before pressing it to his, her hand caressing his cheek. Ice melted against her palm, water trickled down her wrist into her sleeve.

"Do you want to call the constable?"

She shook her head. "He'll be busy. I'll be fine once we're home."

He scanned the street over her head. "Whatever it is, feels off and we shouldn't lead them to your place. Come back to my hotel." The wind shifted, swirling through the streets in the opposite direction, carrying the scent of sulfur with it. "You're definitely not going home. Let's go."

He pivoted, arm around her, picking up their pace, turning at the next intersection. That stretch of street had two burnt out lights before the next corner.

They hurried, mindful of the slippery sidewalk.

Along the darkest stretch, an inky shape darted across their path, startling them.

Olivia's foot skid sideways, forcing her to collide with Nick, who caught her before they both went down.

Distracted, the shape veered back, growing as it arced toward them, billowing.

Olivia's lungs froze, denying her air as she flinched away.

Her gut twisted against the overwhelming forces of hatred and despair crowding her, dragging at her heart.

Nick's hand shot out, freezing the oily black cloud inches before it touched them.

Sulfuric anguish floated toward them, caught on the frigid winds.

"Jésus," Olivia finally gasped, eyes wide.

"What the fuck is that?" he breathed. "Hurry." He dragged her off the sidewalk onto the road before the thing reanimated. He lifted his hand as it crackled to life, freezing it again as he instinctively pulled Olivia toward the light at the end of the road.

He turned to with one last flick of his hand to hold it in place before they rounded the corner toward a busy street with brighter street lights.

They didn't speak again until they reached Nick's hotel, glancing over their shoulders every few minutes. If the thing followed, it did so unseen.

He practically shoved her into the ambient lobby, dragging her toward the elevator, hand clamped around hers, securing her to him as though his body could shield hers from such a creature.

As soon as he ushered her into the room, he ensured the black out curtains were drawn across the window and flicked on every light in the limited space.

They faced each other, chests rising and falling until they exploded at once.

"What the heck was that?" Olivia burst out.

Nick demanded, "have you encountered one of those before? It looked like it was targeting you."

"Me? Why would it come for me? I've haven't had any trouble until you suddenly showed up in town."

Love and a warning.

She flicked 'love' away from her mind to concentrate on the 'warning'.

'I have zero interest in love, as it always comes with large blaring danger signals.' She'd said to Quinn.

Olivia suppressed a nervous giggle as she watched Nick considered her words.

He ran a hand over his thick hair then down his substantial beard as he paced the short stretch from wall to entrance. "Could it be what she was talking about? The balance in jeopardy during the Ascension?"

"You're speaking words but I have no idea what you're saying, Nick."

He paused, gaze landing on Olivia. "No. That can't be it. Your Mr. Anderson smelled of sulfur when I put him in the cruiser. It's got to be connected to you."

Olivia balked. "What the heck? No way. I'm a nobody. I go to work, I do volunteer work, I go home. Wash, rinse, repeat. That's it." She jabbed an accusatory finger in his direction. "You, on the other hand is Mr. Santa Claus himself. Jolly old Saint Nick, the ultimate Do-Gooder of the planet and it's right before Christmas."

Nick grunted at that, scowling.

"Anderson attacked you, Olivia. That thing billowed toward *you*, before I froze it."

"And what was *that*, anyway? You can control time or something?"

"Don't change the subject, Liv. You're the target, I'm sure of it."

"You can manipulate time, and *I'm* the target? You're not making any sense."

"It makes perfect sense," he countered.

"Wha—why?" Olivia threw her hands up, dropping them on her thighs.

He stared at her, eyes wide, lovely lips compressed as thoughts ticked through his mind. He finally blinked.

"You can't go home."

"Excuse me?" Olivia planted her hands on her hips. "Of course I'm going home, I have to—work tomorrow. Some of us have to pay rent."

Work on finding a new job.

The frown line between Nick's brows deepened as he stared at Olivia.

"I'll just go in the morning. Your flight is tonight, isn't it? I'll cover the room cost when I check out."

"Come with me. It would only be for a short while. Till Christmas morning. Then we'll resolve this. Somehow."

Olivia gaped. "I—wha—that's crazy. I can't. I wouldn't get through airport security. My passport is at home and I don't have anything packed."

"You won't need a passport, and we'll take care of anything you'd need once we're there."

Olivia lifted a brow. "You can manipulate airport security too?"

Nick grunted. "No, of course not. We're not going to the airport." He turned away, checking throughout the room as he gathered the last of his belongings and tucked them into a leather satchel. "My ride's meeting me on the roof."

"Holy crap, Nick—you can't just land a helicopter on the roof of any building you like in this city."

"We're not traveling by helicopter," he glanced at his watch. "Just a few more hours then we can mount up."

"Mount up?" Olivia's hands clutched her hair as all of the images she'd ever seen advertised of Santa Claus rolled through her mind. "Please tell me we aren't flying in a sleigh to the North Pole. I don't think I—,"

Nick snorted. "Sleipnir doesn't like sleighs, they're too bulky." He secured the satchel and set it by the door. "Really, Olivia, I didn't think you'd buy into the propaganda. Does your djinn friend live in a lamp or ride a magic carpet?"

"Well, not exactly—,"

"Do you have a portrait stashed away some place that ages for you?"

"Of course not, that's creepy."

"Bathe in milk—or better yet, the blood of virgins to preserve your ageless beauty?"

"Nick!" Olivia laughed finally noticing the twinkle in his eye. "Okay, point taken. But you've got my curiosity afire now."

"You'll see. If you come with me."

"Will I be warm enough?" She glanced down at her winter attire.

"I'll keep you warm."

When she lifted her gaze to his, she blushed from her forehead down to her toes at the look in his eyes, desire flooding her body. The bed loomed nearby.

Suddenly far too hot, she unbuttoned her jacket, setting it aside. "That thing didn't seem to like light and they're all on in here. You've said we have a few hours to till... Sleipnir is it, arrives?"

Nick nodded, shrugging out of his own jacket, laying it atop hers. "I think we'll be safe here." He opened his arms to her.

Without a single thought to resist, she instantly moved into his embrace, whispering against his warm chest. "What a night. Weekend, really."

"It has been eventful." His low voice rumbled against her ear.

"Friday was... crappy. Yesterday I thought would be a magical one night and I'd never see you again. This evening we negotiated a once a year date and now you're talking about whisking me away. It's all so surreal."

"You speak as though you haven't had much contact with the paranormal world."

"I haven't. I've lived as far under the radar as I could. Barring actual invisibility, it's the best way to survive. If no one knows you exist, no one can bother you."

Nick leaned back, hand cupping Olivia's cheek to draw her gaze to his face.

"I certainly know you exist and I plan to bother you as much as I can now that I know it."

She smiled, rubbing her cheek into his hand then turned and kissed his palm.

Heart pounding in her chest, she closed her eyes. "It's all just so fast. I'm not used to any of this."

Nick chuckled. "Aside from delivery night, nor am I. Nothing changes much over the centuries. We just to our thing, day to day. I don't think we're all that much different."

"You'll tell me about it?"

"If you're coming, we'll show you all of it." His thumb drifted over her cheekbone. "And we'll figure out what the deal is with that black cloud. I can't leave you here alone and at risk. Especially if it's my fault." Nick's gaze caressed Olivia's features.

"It isn't. How can you say that?"

"Don't worry about it. We'll fix it, though." He dipped his head to taste her lips.

Olivia had no idea how either of them could 'fix' a thing like that, but she wasn't going to waste this new-found time with Nick dwelling on it.

She immediately opened to him, sliding her tongue across his in invitation.

He growled against her mouth, lifting her into his arms and carried her to the bed as he had the night before.

She'd thought there'd only be one night and was suddenly gifted with another. She was going to savour it.

Olivia's hands were in a flurry to pull his shirt up over his head and unbuckle his belt, needing him, wanting his skin against hers again. She slid her hand into his jeans as his mouth traveled down her neck.

He pushed her shirt up over her head, nuzzling her breasts.

Over her, he met her lips, kissing her deeply as he pressed his bare chest to hers, arms cradling her.

He throbbed in her hand as she gently stroked him, slowing their fevered pace.

They didn't have all night, but they did have some time and she didn't want to go too quickly. This time was a boon and she had to make the most of it.

She still reeled from the sudden turn of events this evening and determined to shut them out for a little longer.

Maybe they'd imagined it. After all, neither had slept much the night before.

She had Nick. For at least a few more hours. That's all that mattered right now.

Opening her eyes she stared into his dark gaze as she wiggled out of her pants.

He did likewise as she unhooked her bra.

Her fingers caressed his length, massaging his tip.

His breath shuddered against the crook of her shoulder. "Liv."

She went up on tiptoe, snaked her arms around his broad tattooed shoulders and slid her legs around his hips, aligning him to her entrance.

He thrust, filling her.

"Nick." She moaned, muscles clenching him tight, arms grasping his wide shoulders.

She'd been in love a few times in her long life—at least she'd thought so at the time.

This—with Nick felt so much different. She wouldn't call it love, it was too quick, too soon.

But certainly... special. Magical.

Intense as it drummed her heart and echoed throughout her body.

Whatever this was between them just clicked together like a magnetic lock and key unable to resist one another.

His hands and lips seemed to be everywhere, all at once as his hard length slid in and out of her, driving her to the edge.

Too soon.

Everything about her time with him seem to reach its end too soon.

She wanted more. She realized in those moments as she reached her peak that she'd always want more, of Nick.

Olivia vowed that, if they did truly meet once a year, she would cherish every second of it.

She gasped, clinging to him.

"Livy, my Livy." He groaned as he buried himself deep and went rigid.

The tenderness in his voice, in his most vulnerable moment, the longing in it made her throat tight.

She recognized the underlying loneliness whispering to her heart.

Catching his breath, he opened his eyes to hers. His fingers caressed her face as he kissed her with so much gentleness for such a large man.

Yes, she would go north with him.

I'd be crazy not to.

Chapter Ten

Nick made love to Olivia again and again, with murmured conversations in between.

He wanted to know everything about her, this woman that had stumbled into his life so suddenly, bringing a light to it that he hadn't known in so long.

He lay stretched out, head on hand, Liv curled into him. He studied every faint freckle on her face, the perfection, and the minute imperfections, that made her unique.

Did she have a family?

No, she told him, just her closest friend, the djinn, Gena, that had gifted her this life.

Long ago, her birth family had sacrificed her to a dragon for the sake of their village—so they'd believed.

Pain flickered in her blue eyes as she whispered "It was for the best. In a long and circuitous way: it led to this moment, though, didn't it?"

"Don't do that. Don't diminish what they did. Just because the dragon turned out to be a shifter doesn't change the fact they believed they were sending you to your death. To save themselves."

"Nick, it was five centuries ago. For the good of the many."

"And you were a child." His intense gaze flicked over her features as he pushed the wisps of hair from her face. "That's why you do it, isn't it? Your work to help the vulnerable? Those cast out of society?"

She swallowed. "It always has been. Convent work, fostering, orphanages wherever I've lived, I've found people in need. Adults, children..." she shrugged.

"And none of your own."

She shook her head.

"Have you? Had children?"

Pain beat in Nick's chest. He nodded.

Her fingers smoothed over his brow.

"I did. A wife, a son, and a daughter, killed in a raid."

"And you never remarried."

He shook his head. "We retaliated—not the children, but all the adults." He sighed, rubbing his eyes. "My worst moment. Our worst moments, led to this path too. Atonement for the orphans we created in our vengeance."

Her fingers trailed along the tattoos adorning his neck. "Still, after all these years?"

"Everything we—I—did? It never seems to be enough. I don't believe it can be. The world has changed so much in the last thousand years. And yet, it really hasn't. People haven't changed."

"I know." Her fingers drifted over his brow. "But it doesn't mean we shouldn't keep trying."

"I'm tired. We're all tired. But I'm glad it's led to these moments, here with you. It is a great solace after so long a time alone."

The nearly inaudible sound of harness bells drew his attention to the present. "Sleipnir is coming. Better dress quickly, he isn't patient."

Olivia rose from the bed, scavenging for her strewn clothing, tossing him his, as she found them.

"You're comfortable around horses?" Nick pulled his shirt over his head, then slipped his feet into his boots.

Olivia dipped behind the bed, one sock in hand while she hunted for the other. "No, they terrify me. My uncle had a mean mare when I was young, so I learned to avoid them."

"That may be a problem."

Her head popped up from behind the bed. Her mouth popped open. "You said there was no sleigh."

He shook his head.

"Really? Ah, crap shots." She slumped against the wall to pull her socks on, casting him baleful looks. "Does he bite? He won't crush my foot with his hooves, will he?"

"He won't. But he may push you around a bit if you let him."

Olivia stood, muttering, as she pulled her boots on. "Wonderful. Not really easing my concerns here, Nick."

He held up her scarf as she moved toward him. Rather than hand it to her, he looped it over her head and shoulders, pulling her closer. He looked down into her large blue eyes as he tucked it into place. His voice turned gruff, "I'll protect you, Liv."

She blinked, concern clearing from her forehead, and smiled.

His throat tightened at the naked trust in her expression as she looked up at him, stirring something he'd thought long ago lost from his heart.

He cleared his throat. "Ready?"

Olivia drew a deep breath and nodded. "Ready."

Nick grabbed his satchel, pulling it over his head and settled it on his shoulder before grabbing Olivia's hand firmly in his and eased the door open. He poked his head out, glancing up and down the empty corridor. "No creepy shadows."

She squeezed his hand, following at his gentle tug, their footsteps light as they hurried toward the stairwell. He guided her up to the top floor.

"Won't it be locked?" She hesitated.

"Pre-arranged agreement with management. They let rooftoppers up here all the time, so long as they sign waivers." He pushed the door open to a glittering panorama of city lights, twinkling in the crisp midnight winter air, the moon low in the western sky. He guided her to a lit corner of the rooftop.

Olivia's breath escaped in a soft puff as she took in the scene of her city from above. "It's so beautiful up here."

The illuminated parliament buildings dominated one side, the black and silvered river rushed along behind it, while the city stretched southward from the front of the grounds.

Olivia shivered. Nick drew her close, wrapping his arms around her, reveling in the feel of her leaning into him as they absorbed the view.

Sleipnir's harness bells grew louder in Nick's inner ear. "He's almost here," he whispered into the soft hair covering her ear.

The wind picked up, swirling the rooftop snow around them. Nick turned to face the center of the roof, waiting for Sleipnir's arrival.

The air surrounding them crackled.

Olivia jumped with a gasp at the sudden pop, right before the city lights surged, the illumination drawn toward an open ring through which Sleipnir became visible.

"Jésus," Olivia breathed.

Chapter Eleven

Sleipnir was the biggest frikking war horse Olivia had ever seen. Ever.

And she'd seen many in her time.

She should have been more shocked by the swirling portal framing him.

Her breath clung inside her chest as she stared into his glowing eyes.

All shades of smoke, soot, and charcoal variated through his coat, down to his hocks. Sigils were carved into the wicked hooves. His thick mane and tail were arranged into elaborately secured braids. He wore saddle, harness and bridle.

She swallowed as she tore her eyes from his, flicking to the muzzle hiding his ferocious teeth, down to the powerful, solid hooves that would not just crush her feet, but leave her in a crumpled mess if he didn't like her.

Nick smiled at the beast, stroking his neck with fondness.

"Uhm, Nick? He's really big. You didn't say he was big, Nick."

"He's magnificent, isn't he? King of all warhorses." Nick's smile slid to concern as he noticed Olivia's trepidation, her gaze remained locked on Sleipnir.

"He's as gentle as a puppy." Nick ran his hand between Sleipnir's eyes to his nose then reached for Olivia's hand.

Liv let out an awkward laugh.

Sleipnir's glowing eyes narrowed on her and he stomped a foot with a huff.

She backed a step.

Nick grasped her hand and pulled her forward. "Liv, this is the only way to get home. You're not staying here with that thing out there targeting you."

"I'm not convinced it's after me. Besides, it's less scary than your horse," she muttered.

Sleipnir grunted.

Turning her attention to Nick's determined face, she blew out a breath. "Okay, sorry, I'm not making a great first impression on your friend." She gave him an awkward pat between the eyes. "Nice to meet you, I'm Olivia."

Sleipnir huffed, turning his big glowing eye to Nick.

"She's nervous." Nick offered. At the jerk of Sleipnir's great head, Nick gathered the reins in one hand, Olivia's hand in the other. "He wants to go."

Not knowing where to start, she stared at the stirrup for several seconds before she was suddenly hoisted by Nick's powerful hands up into the saddle. He settled in behind her, adjusting his satchel as he secured his feet in the stirrups and reins in his hands to either side of Olivia.

Her heart pattered as she looked out over the city skyline from atop Sleipnir, the portal crackling around them, dimly wondering if—when—she'd be back.

Of course I will, and soon. It's just a quick visit...

She yelped as Sleipnir jerked into motion. Colour and air crackled and swirled, building into a rushing storm around them as Sleipnir ran toward the edge of the hotel roof.

Olivia drew breath to scream as she slammed herself backward into Nick's solid chest, preparing for the inevitable drop.

The scream hovered in her throat as Nick's left hand dropped the leather strap, his strong arm locking her against him.

The instant sense of comfort and safety stayed the panic as Sleipnir's powerful body launched them into the air. The expected drop didn't follow.

Her chest rose and fell, trying to pump oxygen to her brain to process what was happening, more terrifying than any of the rollercoasters she'd stupidly convinced herself to try.

The faster that Sleipnir's hooves worked, the more of the city skyline disappeared into the crackling storm of colour enveloping them.

Seconds later, the bunching of his muscles slowed, and the colours and rush of air around them did likewise, dissipating to a very different scene.

Now on solid, snow covered ground, they cantered toward an ice-layered mountain with the Aurora Borealis dancing in the star strewn sky above.

Sleipnir's portal continued to fizz around them as he carried them toward the pristine snow-covered peaks.

Olivia's breath eased out in a great puff, crystallising in the frigid air causing the end of her nose to prickle. "It's so beautiful."

Distracted by the sight overhead, Olivia was late to notice the unveiling of massive double doors ahead.

She blinked, adjusting to the appearance of an entrance embedded in the mountainside that hadn't been there seconds before.

As they approached, heavily rune carved stone pillars formed to either side of the doors, which slowly swung open. More pillars lined the path within, supporting the mountain's maw and gullet from collapsing.

The sound of Sleipnir's hooves transitioning from crunching snow-covered ground to stone path was jarring as the cavern echoed everything around them.

Firmly inside the cave, the doors swung closed behind them. The charged air of Sleipnir's portal fell away and torches affixed to the pillars flickered to life with an unearthly glow, similar to the Aurora Borealis outside.

Olivia maintained her silence as she adjusted to Sleipnir's movement. Nick's arm no longer crushed her to him, but still held her firmly in place atop his steed.

"Is this the north pole?" Olivia's voice ricocheted back to her over the sharp clack of Sleipnir's hooves.

"In a sense, it is."

"Cryptic."

Nick grunted.

The Associate's gaze fixed on the hotel roof line where the sky above it crackled to life.

Fuck.

She instantly began a spell to augment her reach.

Enraged by the pawn's failure to remove the influence of this human woman reported to be of keen interest to her target, she'd had to take matters into her own hands and risk exposure.

What she hadn't counted on was recognizing the woman's face through the taint's vision as it bore down on her. Nor the target's ability to hold the magical creature at bay.

She'd tracked them through the streets, nearly losing them in the downtown sector when she was forced to hang further and further back to avoid detection, forced to alter her plan.

They won't be happy.

Focusing on her spell before the portal closed, she whispered the incantation faster.

She needed to figure out how to tip the target in their favour.

She couldn't risk the hotel security cameras identifying her, so she'd stayed to the shadows, watching the main lobby door from across the road, waiting, watching, for some opportunity.

She'd sent a Taint up the side of the building, seeking, unable to find something to latch onto.

Now, monitoring the progress of the crackling portal, she pushed her magic into the spell, gauging her timing.

It would have been so much easier, if she'd been able to hook onto one of them in the darkened street when they'd left the old church, infecting them with a few spores. Then she'd be able to track them anywhere.

Except when they left this realm. Then it was harder—though not impossible.

Especially now, with the alignment accelerating the Ascension, the veils thinned, enabling access throughout the many realms connected to this world.

Still, this new complication would have to be dealt with. The plan couldn't change.

The spell she launched skyward, a roiling black froth, hovered at the brink of the portal's edge.

She caught sight of the giant horse leaping off the side of the hotel roof, the inky spell caught in its wake as the portal slammed closed.

The magic dragged at the Associate as it travelled off world, toward her primary pawn. The one that she'd been tasked to handle for these last few decades.

Like a grappling hook cast through the portal, this spell should enhance the thread beyond, strengthening the link through the deep meditation or dream states.

Her employers wanted access now, and she wanted to take her place, rising up through the ranks.

Now. This solstice period. They refused to wait another year. Their plans were multi-pronged and designed to keep the wardens busy on all fronts.

Waiting another year, or decade, could lose them the element of surprise.

The council had received a warning, but they couldn't know when or how or who would strike them down.

The enemy couldn't be in all places at once.

And this was a precious target.

This woman could tip the target on the wrong side of the Ascension for us, causing us to lose the advantage until the next cycle.

The Associate was confident she could handle it. She had her means.

Not in all this time—all these centuries—had they been discovered.

Her pawn in the other world was a powerful player. She just needed to guide him through her employers' delicate steps to assure the timing and execution was perfect.

Now was her time to shimmer. To prove herself worthy.

Chapter Twelve

Olivia's questions bombarded Nick as they cantered forward.

Instead of answering most of them, he slid his hand over hers, stroking her fingers as Sleipnir carried them home.

He reveled in the feel of her in the saddle before him, giving him the excuse to keep his arms around her. He inhaled the scent of her hair, of her.

Unable to resist, he tipped her chin up toward him with a finger, leaning so that he could kiss her. The questions fell away as she sighed against his lips.

He had questions of his own.

Was he right to bring her here?

What would she think of their home—or their work?

She'd said she would take it over so that he could retire—what would she think of the offer now?

How would she react to his crew—his family? His home?

She had seemed to accept Sleipnir readily enough, once Nick had touched her, calmed her fears, with hooves firmly on the ground again.

Reassured her with his presence and contact.

How would his crew react? He'd never brought anyone home before.

Nick swallowed. He couldn't stay in her world for longer than a few days, how would she fare in his?

Maybe this was a bad idea...

But, this was *their* idea. Wasn't it?

What were they thinking? What was *he* thinking?

He deepened the kiss, needing more of Olivia before they reached this new threshold.

Just a few more moments.

He ignored the desire growing in his lower half the instant his lips met hers, and focused on the upper half.

The sense of peace she gave him when he touched her.

Sleipnir halted.

Nick released Olivia's lips.

She smiled up at him as she opened her sparkling eyes to his, whispering, "The more you do that, the more I want you to."

The pad of his thumb stroked her cheek as he nodded to the scene before them.

She gasped, her hands tightening on his as she took in their rolling expanse of groves backlit by the northern lights. Specks of glittering cosmic dust drifted between the two, pollinating the vast, ancient orchard.

"Oh, Nick. It's so beautiful."

The sound of her raw emotion burrowed into his heart.

He smiled and leaned his knee into Sleipnir's side, signaling him to continue forward.

Olivia didn't know where to look first.

Nick's arms remained locked around her, providing a solid sense of safety atop his massive horse.

She hadn't known what to expect—doing her best to clear her thoughts of all of the Christmas movies, minstrel's tales and songs, commercials, and story books she'd ever seen and just absorb what was before her.

This was not the winter wonderland the stories predicted.

There was no snow at all.

She could never have dreamed up such a sight.

Olivia drew a breath. "This—what—wow." She exhaled.

Speechless, her gaze followed the road extending forward from Sleipnir's great hooves.

The mountain tunnel opened into a vast valley sprawled before them, with the opposite mountain ridge a visible sweep in the distance.

The genesis of a long dormant volcano or comet crater?

A forest of ancient trees of all sizes and types filled the land-scape, with all manner of green and brown and ruddy hues, glittering with the brilliant colours of the Aurora Borealis clinging to their crowns.

Several clearings were visible, and illuminated in a soft amber glow were dwelling houses clustered in tiny hamlets and small villages.

She drew another breath. "Oh, Nick. It's so beautiful."

Behind her, Nick unzipped his jacket. The mountain tunnel had held a deep chill, but here, the valley was like an autumn dawn where the northern lights didn't hover high overhead. They descended to mingle with the trees.

Nick's knee nudged Sleipnir's side, urging him forward.

At a junction in the path, they turned toward one of the hamlets.

"How is this possible?"

Nick's arms lifted around her in a shrug. "Otherworld magic."

Olivia gasped. "Which one?"

"Who knows? It's well protected though. That's our job. Keep it safe and healthy. Though nothing ever happens here."

"And here I thought you spent a whole year making toys that you deliver to kids in one night."

"Not quite. We deliver the seeds that the trees shed that aren't needed for cultivation. The magic happens after I'm gone on to the next place."

"Like wishing trees?"

Nick grunted.

"Wishes for the worthy?"

"For every child. We have no control over what the seed becomes once it leaves my satchel. And no, I don't know how it works. Or why."

As they approached the cluster of buildings, hearth smoke tickled her nose, drawing her attention to the nearest chimney.

She didn't ask anymore questions, opting to study more of her surroundings. Stone and wood-carved homes plunked at random angles along the cobbled path.

Sleipnir halted when a barrel-chested, fully bearded man, a little shorter than Olivia, rounded the corner of a house, frowning at some tool in his hands. Startled by the horse's girth, he looked up at Nick. His eyes flicked to Olivia and a slow grin split his impressively elaborate beard. "Successful party?"

"Enjoyable." Nick grunted.

The man's gaze returned to Olivia, brow lifted as his grin turned flirtatious. "Well if you don't want her, I'll take her and keep her warm and busy."

Heat infused Olivia's cheeks at his expression.

"Thank you, Cupid. But unnecessary." Nick eased himself down from Sleipnir's back, then slipped his hands around Olivia's waist to help her dismount, dragging her along his torso for support.

Olivia's cheeks blazed brighter at the physical reminder of her intimate time with Nick.

"Good," Cupid chuckled. "I'll tell Vixen you're back, she'll want to meet your woman. Everyone else is still in the groves."

"Oh, I'm not his woman. We're just—," Olivia's words rushed after him, but he'd already disappeared. She turned back to Nick. "I don't know what we are."

But the words settled into her as she looked into Nick's eyes. *'Your woman.'*

He held her gaze, expression thoughtful for a few seconds before he approached Sleipnir to remove his gear.

She watched him work, removing the heavy riding gear from the giant horse.

'Your woman.'

Olivia shivered as the words worked their way through her, tempting. Enticing.

Not realistic.

Not that any of this *is anywhere near realistic.*

A light snort escaped Olivia.

I'm five hundred years old and my best friend is a genie.

She sighed.

I have a life in the city, in *the world. His life is here.*

They would have once a year. Maybe.

As her gaze followed his fluid movements, her heart whispered that it wouldn't be enough. She'd had a taste of him.

I should be content with that. It was only supposed to be one night, and I've had two.

But as she watched, she wanted nothing more than to touch him again. To return to the circle of his arms.

"All finished, my friend." His voice was low as he ran a hand along Sleipnir's muscled neck. "I'll see you in a few days."

Sleipnir grumbled low in his throat as he dipped his head before cantering off toward the trees.

Turning back to Olivia, Nick lifted his upturned palm toward her.

Without thinking, Olivia slid her fingers over the rough calluses, following as he led her toward a long house tucked behind the cottages.

He pushed one of the massive doors open with his free hand. Her gaze swept the great hall with its central hearth. Every beam and pillar was carved with intricate animals amid twisting knots. Long wooden tables led to a short riser, where two large chairs faced the entrance. The scent of food drew her further inside, making her mouth water.

"Are those for the king and queen?" Olivia leaned toward Nick, voice hushed as she nodded toward the empty chairs.

His gaze followed hers. "They were. No one sits there anymore, though. Hungry?" He moved toward the central hearth, where a cauldron hung over crackling embers.

"Famished."

"Good. Dash makes the best stew." Nick drew a wooden bowl from a nearby stack and ladled thick stew into it.

"Dash?"

"Our master chef. No recipes, just throws a dash of whatever he thinks of into the pot and it comes out perfect every time." Nick winked as he handed her the bowl and spoon before ladling some for himself.

She moved toward the nearest bench, inhaling the savory fare as she sat. The spoon, was also made of wood, its handle delicately etched with a tree in bloom. Blowing gently on the steam, she waited until Nick was seated before tasting. Flavour exploded across her tongue. "Mmm."

"Thor's balls, it worked!"

Olivia nearly choked on her food at the thunderous words rolling through the vast room from the door behind her. Dropping her spoon, she turned to see three tall figures approaching.

"Sleipnir let us know we had company."

"Glad to see our hard work has paid off," the loud one said with a wide grin.

Olivia gaped at the three giants, easily seven feet tall, with bluish skin and long pointed ears.

"You'll get use to Donder, he doesn't have a volume setting. This is Blixem. They're cousins on my mother's side." Nick said, indicating the second figure with a long jagged scar down the side of his face.

She reached out a hand to shake, eyes darting between the two identical faces of the still grinning giants.

"I expect you haven't met Alfar before," Blixem grinned. "Few have, but you'll get used to us. The others did. After awhile."

"Alfar?" Olivia whispered to Nick.

Before he could answer, the third stepped out from behind the twins, his expression far less friendly than his companions. "The human idea of elves." He explained.

"My brother, Rudolph."

"Half brother." Rudolph sniffed, reddened nostrils curling as he ignored Olivia's proffered hand before turning his attention to Nick, voice nasal. "Wonderful. So you managed to find yourself a willing human. Or did you have to throw it over your shoulder kicking and screaming, like the old days?"

Where the twins were muscled, Rudolph was a larger, leaner and bluer version of Nick. And smelly. Rancid fumes of body odor and stale alcohol emanated from him, threatening Olivia's delicate sense of smell.

"I'm Olivia." She dropped her hand, straightening her shoulders, flicking her attention from Rudolph to the others.

"I don't care."

"Dolph, don't be a dick." Blixem snapped, heading toward the stew pot. "Eat something before you make a complete ass of yourself. Then go take a bath."

Dolph grunted as he turned away from them, and poured himself a drink from a sideboard.

Relieved that Dolph had put more distance between them, Olivia drew a deeper breath to clear the foul smell from her nose and control her instant dislike of Nick's family member.

"Blix and I finished pruning the eastern grove. Tools are with Vixen for sharpening. She'll be here in a minute."

"Thanks Don. Cupid will be pleased to hear we're all on task."

"Everyone else is in the far groves, harvesting. They'll be back in a day or two." Blix straddled a bench, digging into his bowl. "Tell us about the party."

"You'd better wait till Vixen is here. She'll have your scrotum if you give us all the details without her." Don said.

Nick rolled his eyes. "I wouldn't dream of it, after all the effort she went to."

"Mm. No that was all Cupid. He was tired of looking at your mopey face for the last few centuries and had enough. The rest of us just chipped in."

"I don't mope," Nick pinned him with his glare, receiving a return eye roll for his effort.

"Not all of us." Dolph poured another drink, then took up a post, leaning against a nearby pillar. "None of my business."

"And yet you're still hanging around for the details." Blix shot back.

"Fuck you, prick. I don't need—,"

"Manners!" Don cracked, shoving a full bowl into Dolph's chest.

Olivia jumped back into Nick. She drew a deep breath to steady her racing heart as the surrounding air thickened.

"We have a guest." The rest of Donder's words rumbled as he tilted his head toward Olivia.

Dolph snorted, putting the bowl down on the nearest table, cup still in hand.

The door opened once more, drawing their attention to two figures striding toward them.

Olivia smiled as Cupid stopped in front of her, gently took her free hand and bent over it, placing a soft kiss on the back of her knuckles. "Now we can have proper introductions."

She stood to greet the woman with him, offering her hand as she'd done with the Alfar.

"Vixen." Her grasp was firm, her gaze studious, as she looked up into Olivia's eyes. "Tools are sharpened and hanging in their places for tomorrow." She released Olivia, turning her attention to the bowl Don handed her before taking a place at the table, pinning Nick with her unwavering stare.

"Better get started," Cupid settled next to her. "My wife is impatient for your news."

Chapter Thirteen

Nick relayed every detail of his weekend in Ottawa, save for the more intimate ones with Olivia.

"You did well, husband." Vixen said to Cupid. "Perhaps things will be more interesting around here."

"She isn't staying."

Olivia blinked, looking from Vixen's hard stare to Cupid's knowing smirk back to Nick's stony expression.

Don and Blix occupied themselves with their bowls.

Dolph refilled his cup.

"I have work to do." Olivia said.

"What do you do?"

"I, uhm.. Well I'm in between jobs right now. New development as of last week. Company downsizing and stuff." She chuckled, dropping her gaze to her hands. "So I have to find a new one."

Nick frowned at the embarrassment colouring Olivia's cheeks.

Dolph snorted, muttering under his breath.

Nick ignored him.

"There's always plenty to do here," Don offered.

"You can stay at Nick's place." Cupid said. "The spare house is full of vermin."

"We don't have vermin here." Nick lifted a brow.

"Dolph's been hanging out there instead of his own cottage."

"What's wrong with your place?" Nick turned to Dolph.

"Got bored. Besides, it's busy season and it's a long walk."

It was Blix's turn to snort. "And all the alcohol stores are kept here, now. The Nisse were getting too liberal with their self-serve. They were going through a barrel a day."

"Looks like Dolph isn't far behind." Don stood, collecting the empty bowls.

"I have to figure out what threatened Olivia last night so that she can go home and get on with her life."

"She can stay here." Cupid insisted.

"She can't. She doesn't belong here." Nick growled.

Cupid shot to his feet, finger wagging at Nick. "I went to a lot of effort to get you that invitation. And look what you brought us home." He splayed his hands, sweeping toward Olivia. "Perfection. And you want to just toss her back. No, Nick. You keep her."

Nick got to his feet, forcing Cupid to glare up at him. "That's not how this works."

Cupid planted his feet, fists on hips as he glared harder. "Mule-headed. This is exactly how this works. She wouldn't be here if it wasn't."

"She wouldn't be here if someone hadn't attacked her to get to me. That's the only reason she's here." Nick snarled.

"Best get me home as soon as possible so that I can sort that out and get on with my life. Can Sleipnir take me in the morning? Or is there some other way to get back?" Olivia's steady voice drew Nick's attention to her strained face.

Nick's irritation with Cupid's antics fizzled into guilt the instant he saw Olivia's expression.

"You think this is about you? Not her?" Vixen spoke up.

Nick's head jerked in a nod. "The warning at council, the sulfuric smell lingering on the human and the shadow in the alley. Olivia lives firmly in the human world and until this weekend has had little interaction with the paranormal."

"But she is a paranormal, by human standards. Otherwise she wouldn't have been at Quinn O'Clery's party."

"And how do you know any of this?" Nick demanded.

Cupid shrugged. "Council talks, I listen."

"Gossip, more like."

"I'm not gifted. I'm just old." Olivia jumped in and rushed on. "And a little sensitive. But most people are sensitive, they just don't know it. There's nothing paranormal about that."

Dolph made a noise from his post.

"That sounds to me like there's a paranormal story in there somewhere," Cupid said.

"Her past is her business. Don't pry." Nick turned to Olivia. "It's the middle of the night for you. You need to rest."

"Want me to reach out to Quinn?" Cupid asked Nick.

"Please. Her hands are tied as to what she can do, but she knows something."

Nick led Olivia out of the hall toward his cottage, keeping a distance between them that hadn't been there before the meeting.

Her presence constantly tugged at him.

He ignored the urge to take her hand. The more he touched her, the more he needed to. And he'd just firmly reminded himself that she wasn't staying when he'd made the statement to the others.

Time to reinforce that.

Giving in to the selfish need to pull her close, wouldn't do either of them any good.

A pang of guilt resurfaced when he recalled her expression.

It wasn't that he didn't want her to stay.

Freya knew that he wanted nothing more than to keep her, close, forever.

But she needed to go back to her life. Not stay entrapped here for eternity, or until the Creators decided what was next for him and his crew.

He wouldn't subject her to their fate.

Which is what Cupid had conspired to do, apparently.

This is what that party was all about. Finding Nick a partner. A wife?

They'd all interfered.

Except Dolph, who never did anything for anyone else.

Nick sighed, lips parted as he halted at his front door. He turned to look at Olivia, meaning to say something.

Apologize?

But the right words wouldn't rise.

He closed his mouth, opened the door, holding it so that she could precede him inside.

She stepped into his home. His personal space that only he had ever lived in. Friends came and went through out the days, but he'd never shared it with anyone on this level.

"Bedroom is through there," he nodded to an open door off the open living space. "I'll sleep here." He indicated the heavy wood carved furniture with it's thick padding and plump cushions.

Olivia's gaze swept the simple cottage, her tone determined. "You've done enough for me. I won't keep you from your bed. I'll sleep out here."

They stared at one another for a long moment.

Neither suggested sharing it.

As they had done right before the journey.

Something changed during their meeting with his crew—his family.

Reality of their situation.

The love haze had finally worn off.

But something else replaced it.

As he looked down into her direct blue gaze, Nick knew right then that he wouldn't reunite with her every year as they'd planned.

I can't.

The longer he was with her, the desire to hold on to her grew more intense.

Even now, with this understanding, his body urged him to pull her into his arms, kiss her sweet lips and carry her into his room and make love to her again and again until he had to set her free.

Even here, her inner glow drew him to her.

He leaned toward her.

Instinct.

This was never supposed to happen.

I was just supposed to go to a party, blow off a little steam before the big rush and get on with the work.

He wasn't supposed to fall in love.

He leaned away.

She broke eye contact to hide the sweep of disappointment pulling at her features.

Olivia pulled off her boots and coat, leaving them by the door. She didn't say another word as she pulled a cushion from one chair, and tucked herself onto the other.

He opened his mouth to insist that she sleep in the bed when she yawned and mumbled from her curled up position.

"This place is beautiful. You have a nice life here, Nick."

"It's not—," but she'd already relaxed into sleep, her breath deep and steady. "A life."

He rubbed the fatigue from his face, then removed his own boots and coat, setting them aside. He sat on the edge of the empty chair watching her sleep for a while.

"It's not living." He whispered. "It's existing."

When her body sagged into deeper sleep, Nick stood, gathered her up in his arms and carried her to his bed, tucking her in.

Leaning over her, he allowed his fingertips the slightest contact to sweep the blond strands from her face, lingering on her cheek.

She turned into the warmth of his palm, mumbling. "Stay with me, Nick."

"I wish I could." His thumb stroked tiny patterns over her cheekbone. "Odin knows that I wish I could."

Nick needed to cut ties with her. Now.

His wife, Hedi, had been trained to fiercely protect her family. And when their enemies came, Nick hadn't been there to stop the brutal destruction, or help her save their children.

Olivia was gentle, soft-hearted and vulnerable.

Nick had no doubt that this black shadow pursuing her was *his* enemy. Not hers.

A woman like her didn't have enemies like that.

A piece of his inner soul whispered to his logical mind.

Shouldn't you keep her close to protect her all the more?

He had to think this through. Who or whatever it was, had already found her when he'd arrived in that alley. Quinn had seen to it that he had.

Maybe the attack and the warning at the council meeting really were two entirely different events.

Was she being pursued because of the good work that she did?

Is she somehow tied to whatever the Ascension is?

No matter how mundane she thinks she is, she's definitely more than human.

Had she always been? Is that why the djinn chose her?

"I need to know more." Nick nodded, gently extracting his hand from her slackened grasp. "In a few hours is soon enough." He stifled a yawn and took up Olivia's spot on the chair.

Chapter Fourteen

Olivia woke with a start, heart pounding, chest shuddering, fingers clenching the thick coverlet twisted around her sweat-slicked body.

Realizing she was in a bed and not being chased by a crazy, scary shadow down a dark alley, she sat up, throwing aside the blanket as she caught her breath.

As her senses aligned to the waking world, Nick's scent filled her deep breaths.

She was alone in the room. His room. His bed.

She drew one final deep breath as everything else rushed back to her, taking in the sparse, yet cozy bedroom. A tapestry adorned one wall, while a carved armoire dominated another. A window paned with warbled glass let in the coloured northern lights dancing across the coverlet.

The fantasy weekend love affair was over.

Back to business Monday.

The change in Nick—the sudden distance he put between them—had made that clear.

She stood, walking to the window, observing the lights through the glass.

Except, I'm still in a fantasy land.

Vastly different from the dragon's cave that started her journey so long ago, yet just as magical.

Her fingers drifted over the glass, with its tiny trapped bubbles, as Cupid and Nick's words circled through her mind, always coming back to Nick's statement.

'She doesn't belong here.'

Do I belong anywhere?

I need to go back. At least I can be of some service to someone back home.

Which I can't do from here, anyway—even if I wanted to stay—which I don't.

Despite Cupid's insistence and the implications, the notion of staying had only danced through her heart for a millisecond. She hadn't ever tried to grasp it. It was absurd.

But it had left a grain behind, just enough to scratch at her awareness.

A new scent tickled her nose, drawing her attention to the open door.

Bacon?

Olivia ran her fingers through her hair, releasing the tangles, then straightened the bed to make it look as though she'd never been there.

At the bedroom door, she took in the sight of Nick cooking by the open hearth. She lingered for a few minutes, observing the concentration on his face as he worked. Her mouth watered as the aroma of bacon continued to fill the cottage. But it was more than just the food that she hungered for.

This snapshot seared into her brain.

Waking up to this. Every morning.

Her heart tripped.

You don't belong here, Olivia.

And if he wanted you, he'd have said so.

She watched him for a few moments longer, then straightened her shoulders and her heart.

She strode toward the washbasin set on a side table. Cleaning her hands, she stationed herself at the table, slicing the loaf of bread he'd set aside in preparation for the toast rack by the fire. "Tell me about your family."

He turned at the sound of her voice, gaze flicking over her features and down to her hands, working on the bread, before turning back to his task. "Butter is in the cupboard. You met most of the crew last night. What you see is what you get. The others will return with their harvest before it goes out."

She looked up, meeting his direct gaze. "What? Do I have dried drool on my face?" She scrubbed her sleeve over her face.

The corner of his lips quirked. "No. You should rest longer."

"How can I, when there's bacon out here?"

Said bacon expressed a prolonged sizzle with a sudden pop. Nick grunted.

"Tell me about your Djinn. Can they help with the shadow threat?"

Olivia's hands stalled over the loaf. "I can't involve her."

Nick turned his whole body toward Olivia, ignoring the vocal bacon. "Why not?"

"It's complicated."

He lifted a brow.

"Do you just randomly ask your magical friends to solve all your problems?"

"I solve my own problems."

"Exactly."

"You can solve magical problems yourself?"

"I haven't exactly had the chance to try, yet, have I?" She glared at him. "Your bacon is burning."

Staring at her a second longer, he spun around to save their breakfast.

Olivia arranged the bread slices on the toasting rack and set it by the hearth. "Besides, our friendship isn't like that. And she has... limitations that affect her magic."

Nick retrieved several eggs from a nearby bowl and held them up.

"Scrambled. Two please."

"I've never heard of a djinn with limitations. But you're still in contact, which is good. If she can't protect you, maybe she can help figure out how to get rid of the threat. She might know what it is."

"I'd rather not involve her at all."

"That's what family does for one another."

"I wouldn't know about that." Her chest tightened as she plucked at the toast, ignoring the return of his stare. She felt it even though she didn't meet his eyes. She felt it in the set of his body.

Nick removed the cast iron pan from the heat and placed it on a thick wooden block atop the table. Wiping his hands on a thin towel, he tossed it aside and watched Olivia as she finished her own task. As soon as she started spreading the butter on the warmed slices, Nick's fingertip slipped under her chin, gently turning her face toward his.

His gaze was intent, giving her no room to turn away. "*We* will figure this out together."

She blinked, trying to hid her vulnerability, but it was too late, he wouldn't allow her to escape the intensity of his determination.

"We'll make it safe for you to go back to your life so that you can continue with all the good that you do in the world."

She finally pulled away. "It isn't much, Nick. A soup kitchen a few days a week, and kindness to those that need it, is easy."

"Not for everyone, it isn't." He resumed plating the food. "Especially for someone who's been doing it as long as you have. That's rare. Special. You're special."

She accepted the plates without a response as he retrieved a French press containing aromatic coffee.

What do I say to that?

"I will ask her if she knows anything." Olivia finally said after several sips of the rich coffee and half her plate had been consumed. "How do I reach out—assuming my cell won't work here?"

Nick shook his head. "It won't. Cupid is our communications guy. We'll go to his place when we're done. He won't have left for the groves yet."

Olivia's chest pattered a lighter staccato, breath held, she asked. "Can I help? In the groves?"

Looking up from his plate and seeing the hope on her face, Nick smiled, eyes twinkling. "Of course. We need all the help we can get. Especially if the Nisse have been into the barrels again."

Olivia laughed, setting her cutlery across her empty plate, reaching for the coffee cup. "What's a Nisse?"

"I'll explain them on our way to Cupid and Vixen's place." He stood, reaching for her plate to stack on his own and setting the dishes aside in a dry sink.

Donning their winter gear, Olivia followed Nick along the cobbled path toward another cottage on the far side of the longhouse.

"The Nisse?" Olivia reminded him, struggling to keep up with his long strides.

"Are meddlesome pests." Dolph's voice met them at a junction in the path, following them. "Where you going?"

Dolph's overpowering stench threatened Olivia's happy stomach. Tensing, she sped toward Nick.

"Cupid's place. And don't ever let them hear you say that, Dolph. They're an indispensable part of this world's economy. Without them, the groves would wither."

"Which happens anyway when they're drunk all the time." Dolph caught up to Nick with a few strides.

Olivia's gut continued to tighten, causing her wonderful breakfast to compress into a hard lump while coffee acid threaten to rise. She turned her face away as she drew a breath to ease the discomfort.

"Their frenzy will pass once they've worked it through their systems. It always does."

"Last time it was the candy they asked us to import, at least with that, they'd just puke it up if they had too much and get on with work. They can't do that if they're passed out in the trees, Nick."

The mental image made Olivia's stomach flip.

Nick finally rounded on his brother. "It will pass. Leave them alone and focus on your own responsibilities."

Dolph grunted, gaze swiveling to Olivia. "Seems to me everyone has some sort of distraction from the boredom of this place. Must be nice to have a soft, warm one."

"Ah, there you are!" Cupid trundled up the path toward them. "You're coming to my place, aye?"

At Nick's nod, he turned, taking over the lead. "I got a message out to Ms. O'Clery and she's going to find her sister, who's currently working a case."

"A case? Is she a detective?" Olivia dodged a loose cobble on the path, keeping up with Cupid's brisk pace, putting more distance between herself and Dolph's rank odor.

"Of sorts." Cupid opened the door to the cottage he shared with Vixen. The layout was much the same as Nick's, with an additional level. There was as much ironwork art in the home as carved detail on the beams and furnishings. "Vixen added her touch." Cupid beamed at the ornate iron piece above the fireplace mantle.

"It's magnificent."

"Aye, my Vixen doesn't just keep our tools sharp. She's the finest blacksmith I've ever known."

"I'm the only blacksmith you've ever known." Vixen descended the stairs, fingers nimbly plaiting her hair. "Did you offer tea?"

"On it." Cupid left Olivia's side to retrieve several mugs and the steaming kettle. "O'Clery said she would need some time and agreed with me that Olivia should stay here with us."

Nick grumbled into the mug Cupid handed him. "Of course she did."

"Under no circumstances is she to go back. Not until we deal with this threat."

"What? I—I can't just stay here indefinitely."

"How long?" Dolph remained standing by the door.

Nick remained silent, staring at the floor.

Cupid shrugged. "As long as it takes. There is no hurry here."

"That's not exactly true—," Nick crossed his arms.

"We have work to do and can't lounge around entertaining this human. Especially not so close to the delivery date." Dolph sneered.

Cupid shoved a hot mug in Dolph's hand, glaring up at him. "No one is lounging. It's tea for five minutes before we go. Sit." He turned back to his tray, giving Vixen a pained look.

Dolph stubbornly remained by the door, but did sip his drink.

"Who can I shadow? Since I can't just take myself home, I will work as much as I'm able. I just don't know anything about trees."

"Nick." Cupid drew out his name when no one answered. Having Nick's attention, he tilted his head, swiveling his eyes in Olivia's direction.

Nice.

It was Olivia's turn to cross her arms over her chest.

Nick blinked and glanced around at the faces, pulled in from his thoughts. "Vixen or the twins. I won't make her suffer Dolph's company. I need you on standby for O'Clery, Cupid."

Dolph snorted.

Not, 'I'd be happy to have Olivia work with me'.

Stung, Olivia drained her mug as she controlled her disappointment.

Fantasy night was long gone.

Cupid gaped, then compressed his lips at Nick's resolved expression. "Fine. But the twins left over an hour ago."

"My tasks today do not require help." Vixen gathered the empty mugs, offering Olivia a gentle smile and a pat on the hand to lessen the rejection. She turned to Nick. "Besides, the Nisse finished off the ale last night."

Nick sighed, rubbing a hand over his face. "I really wish the Council wouldn't schedule the gathering during my quarter."

"What's done is done. Off you go." Vixen opened the door to usher everyone out. "Dash will be back to prepare lunch."

"Is there another way to go back? Other than Sleipnir?" Olivia whispered.

Vixen shook her head. "Not that we know of, at this time."

"At this time? What does that mean?"

"Olivia?" Nick called from outside the door.

She glanced between Vixen and the front door and rushed after Nick who didn't appear to have noticed she wasn't right behind him.

The last thing she needed was to get lost in the forest.

At least it wasn't bitter cold and snowing here.

"Watch your step," Nick tossed over his shoulder just in time for Olivia to side step a small arm and a leg sprawled out from under the bushes lining the walk to Cupid and Vixen's cottage.

Unconcerned, Nick hadn't slowed his stride.

Nisse?

She was torn, wanting to stop and inspect the inert creature to ensure it wasn't harmed, but Nick had reached the edge of the trees where the path darkened between them.

Best go in case he leaves the path.

She cast a last glance at the arm and leg before dashing after the blond giant.

Chapter Fifteen

Dolph dropped his empty mug on the tray Vixen held out before him, ignoring her pinned stare.

"What?"

"You haven't set foot in this house in decades."

"And?"

Her eyes narrowed on her upturned face. "What are you up to?"

"Curiosity." He shrugged. "Don't see many new faces around here anymore."

"You can't stand humans."

"And?" he prompted again.

"And you know as well as everyone else here that she is meant for Nick. He just needs time to adjust."

Dolph's laugh was abrupt. "You two are meddlesome. Neither of them look interested in your matchmaking."

Vixen lifted a brow. "Says the cranky Alfar poking his blue nose in where it wasn't before." She set the tray aside, planted her hands on her hips and increased the intensity of her stare. "What are you up to?"

"Nothing. That human shouldn't be here at all, and I want her gone already."

"Mhmm."

Dolph backed toward the still open door as Cupid finished his task, preparing to leave. "I will accompany you back to the tower. I'm going that way, anyway."

Cupid appeared startled by Dolph's announcement as he looked between him and his wife. "What's going on?"

Vixen shrugged, finally turning away. "Maybe you can find out. And mind the Nisse. They're still sprawled in the bushes and are a tripping hazard. Should have planted those junipers further away from the path." She grumbled, retrieving the tea tray. "I'll be in the forge till lunch."

Cupid kissed her cheek on his way by. "Be sure to tell Dash we have an indefinite guest. He'll want to make something special."

Dolph ground his teeth as he hovered by the front door, waiting for the dwarves to finish their domestic dawdling and get on with the business of the day.

Deciding to put some distance between himself and their repulsive affectionate exchange, he resisted the urge to kick at the splayed Nisse passed out on the edge of the path.

Nuisance. Always getting into things and barely doing anything useful, despite what Nick claims.

Dolph clenched his fists.

Odin knows I hate it here. Hate everything about this place, and especially hate everyone in it.

And now there's a fucking human. How much worse can it get? A human. Layered punishment, surely.

From the path junction, he glanced back toward the cottage where Vixen stood, watching him.

I need to be more careful. She notices too much.

Or work faster. At least her husband is more oblivious.

"Alright, Dolph, what are ye up to? You never accompanied me anywhere." Cupid demanded, as Dolph fell instep alongside him.

"Why are you and that wife of yours so suspicious? A new face shows up and suddenly my curiosity is suspicious?"

"You didn't make this much effort the last time anyone from outside appeared and we all know how you feel about humans."

"I told you last night, I'm bored."

Cupid grunted as he turned onto the tower path.

"Besides, isn't it risky leaving the frequency open?"

"Aye, but I'll keep my eye on things, as I always do. The crystals are set. Nothing will get in." He spun on Dolph, eyes narrowed on him as Vixen's had been. "The Grove will be safe. I won't let anything in to infect it. We all know how important it is to the Balance. So you'd best be off to tend your thicket. There is much to be done, and while the Grove is important, this task is too." Cupid waved Dolph off in the opposite direction of the fork he meant to take.

Dolph glanced up at the column of the tower rising from beyond this section of ash trees.

"Maybe someday, if you prove yourself to the Gods, we'll all be able to move on from this place. Until then, you best get to work. And take a bath."

Dolph bit back a retort as the dwarf turned his back on him.

He pinched his eyes against the pressure in his head. The nagging insistence to keep to the plan, invading his dreams so that he couldn't even rest in peace.

He huffed at that. Rest in peace?

Yeah, not in over a millennium.

He drew a breath, straightening his shoulders.

Patience.

Chapter Sixteen

Nick cast a final glance over his shoulder at his brother, lingering at the door, and distantly noted Olivia's tight expression as she stepped out of the cottage to follow him.

Guilt tightened his gut further.

Something isn't right.

But he couldn't allow himself to close the distance he was trying to put between Olivia and himself.

He couldn't—wouldn't keep her.

Everyone's treating her like a Christmas puppy under the tree.

She had to go back.

Olivia didn't belong in this place. She belonged in the living world, not this in-between place.

His heart swelled at the notion that his crew conspired to find him someone special, having reached out to one of the Fates for help.

I can't.

I don't deserve it.

She doesn't deserve this existence.

But fate had indeed put someone in front of him, sent her stumbling into him that very night.

And she is perfect.

All the more reason to figure out how to get her safely home.

Safe.

What were those sulfuric things? Who would send them? Surely they're connected to the events that O'Clery's sister had warned them against.

A bid to infect the grove?

It had gone after Olivia.

Infect her, infiltrate the grove and ruin them?

Or hurt her to impede Nick's ability to do the work?

"Odin's teeth!" He growled, increasing his pace.

"Nick?" Olivia's voice drew him back.

He spun around to see her rushing to keep up with his much longer strides.

She stopped short when her gaze landed on his face. She swallowed.

"I'm sorry."

"What the hell for?"

Her shoulders rose, palms up. "For... this. All of this. Me being here. My presence is disrupting things when you all have so much to do. I would go back, Nick. Just help me do that."

"I can't." His shoulders dropped as he realized his tension was putting her on edge. "And don't be sorry, none of this is any fault of yours."

"Sure." Heavy with disbelief, her voice fell flat, as she shrugged, turning her gaze to the trees. "Where do we start?"

"Through here." He led her to a cart waiting in the middle of a small clearing.

He ignored the tug on his chest as he caught the wonder returning to her lovely features when she turned her blue gaze up to the lights dancing over their heads. The wavering blues and greens made her eyes sparkle with such delight that it only enhanced her beauty.

"It's so beautiful," she whispered.

Nick had been long immune to the sight of the Aurora Borealis pollinating the grove. He'd forgotten his own reactions to it from those distant early days. The sky could be blue, grey, brown—it no longer mattered.

Until now. Somehow, Olivia made it matter. She renewed the sense of wonder, like she peeled away the layers of film that had grown over his awareness. The deeply mundane repetition of their days, that weren't even really days.

They cycled through sectors of time in this place that operated differently from earthly time. They still behaved as though their bodies required the sleep and sustenance of humanoid life, existing as 'other'.

"There is a basket in the corner of the cart for seed collection." He retrieved the basket, looping its leather strap over her shoulder so that the reed weave would rest against her hip. Leading her toward the trees, he scanned for which looked ready for their collection. "Here, see how the upper branches droop. It's ready for us."

He hesitated before reaching out to grasp her delicate fingers. The contact sent a gentle surge up through him. Resisting the ever-present desire to pull her into his arms, he allowed himself the simpler act of sliding his fingers between hers as he pressed her palm to the tree's trunk. Standing behind her, he smoothed his other hand along her wrist, turning her palm up, cradled within his. He murmured next to her ear, inhaling the scent of her hair. "Just be still."

She stood, silent, face upturned to the crown, watching the branches sway over head.

Nick closed his eyes against the need to kiss her, to close his fingers over hers and pull her into his chest while he buried his face in her hair and the crook of her delicate neck.

He smiled when she gasped and slowly opened his eyes, knowing what she saw.

"It's so vibrant!"

A single speck of blue light drift down from the tangle of branches and leaves, floating toward her palm. It surged, expanding its aura as it came into contact with Olivia's palm before settling in the valley of her fingers, where it pulsed like a purring kitten.

"I've never seen one do that before." He guided her hand to the basket, allowing it to settle with a small tumble into the milkweed fluff lining the bottom.

"Everyone does this?"

"Not everyone. Dolph never touches the seeds, so he tends to other jobs. Some of the other dwellers also prefer other tasks.

Dolph hadn't tried to harvest since that first time a seed touched his palm and withered. To Nick's knowledge, he hadn't tried again.

"There are more coming," Olivia's breath hitched as she drew their still-linked hands up to catch the yellow, green and pink seeds descending toward them. She tucked them into the basket with the blue one. "They're so warm and soft."

He remained at her back as more fell toward her palm. The pure delight in her gasps and the glow of her face stretched his heart. When she leaned back into him he was nearly undone.

A flash of what could be.

Here, with her in his arms, collecting the seeds as he reveled in her delight. And he knew that delight would be eternal. She would never allow such a thing to become mundane and would cherish every touch of the sacred grove as though it were the first.

It was her way.

Maybe she was meant to be here too? With him? Or to succeed him so that he could move on?

But the idea of moving on no longer interested him, where remaining here, with Olivia did.

No.

She needs to go back. The world needs her kindness from within. Trapped here, she would never be able to do that.

His thumb stroked the back of her hand before he released her, stepping away.

Every time he was too near, he was unable to resist the draw and found himself grasping for her.

Distance.

"When this one is done, the next will be waiting for you."

"Where are you going?" She watched as he shed his jacket and shirt, draping both over the side of the cart before retrieving an ax.

"There is an oak nearby that is actively dying. We prune the dead branches to ease its strain until it is done. After that, we will remove it to make room for its offspring to rise."

Nick didn't miss the slide of her gaze over his bare chest, or the sudden blush that made her cheeks glow as bright as the pink seeds.

He had to work her out of his system before he gave in to his need for her and pulled her back to him.

"Mind the seeds, I'll be back soon." He nodded to the purple one drifting toward her palm.

As soon as she turned to catch it, Nick ducked away, a smile tugging at his lips.

With Nick's warm chest at her back, Olivia's heart had bloomed with every tiny fluff of light that touched her palm. Each a gentle caress of energy in which she *felt* its potential, its excitement to *be*.

They were living things.

The seeds of a special type of magic, fostered here.

Are there other places like this? Is it the only one in all the universe? Surely not?

And then Nick was gone again.

Though the seedlings continued to shine just as bright, they didn't seem to trill on her palm the way they had when Nick touched her—or them. Whichever it was. They seemed to react to his presence and so too, to his absence.

She glanced over her shoulder as he divested himself of his coat and shirt, muscles taut as he drew an ax from the cart.

Olivia's mouth went dry at the sight.

His fist gripped the haft just below the intricately etched ax head. The soft lights from the sky and trees wavered across the tattoos adorning his muscled chest and arms. Her gaze dropped to his pants, slung low on his trim hips. He deftly spun the ax in his hand, adjusting his grasp. An unconscious thing to do—an effortless habit.

Oh, my.

She swallowed. Dimly, his words sank in and she returned her attention to the falling seedlings.

When she glanced back again, he was gone. Clenching her eyes tight, she drew a deep breath, desperate to purge herself of the sudden surge of desire at the sight of him.

Focus, Liv.

She bit her lip, watching the progress of the tumbling specks of light, her thoughts returning to Nick. After a while she gave up trying to keep him out and just allowed her mind free rein.

Nick, bare chested with the ax. Nick cooking breakfast. Awakening to Nick's scent in his bedroom, the hotel room, the guest room at Quinn's manor.

The feel of his hands on her body that made her feel worshipped and precious. Safe. The taste of his lips and tongue, the warmth of his body against hers, sliding over her—into her.

His hard body and soft touch. The twinkle in his eye when he let go of the intensity of his gaze.

The way he looked at her. Sometimes heated, sometimes with longing that made her ache all the more for him.

Her breath hitched as her body flushed with need. Her heart clenched, knowing that it wasn't going to be.

They'd had two magical nights.

But she wanted more. So much more.

Greedy, Liv.

This is it. Once I go home, this will be the last I see of him.

There wouldn't be the yearly reunion that they'd playfully planned. She knew it deep down to her toes.

It wasn't just the desire. She found comfort in his proximity. Being close to him made her tummy flutter at the same time it gave her peace.

Being wrapped in his arms felt... right.

This is it.

Returning her attention to the task before her, she watched the tree's branches lift as the seeds detached. After a time, they stopped coming, with the rest content to remain as they were.

She moved on to the next tree, a pine, testing. Its branches didn't droop and nothing descended. On to the next giant, a banyan with sagging limbs, the seeds tumbled faster than she expected, drawing her full attention. The heat emanating from the seeds and trees warmed her so that she unbuttoned her coat and eventually removed it.

Finally, when she could barely keep the seeds balanced so that they didn't overflow the basket, she carefully placed it in the cart where Nick had been back to add fallen dead wood and cut logs.

Even now, divested of the basket, her body buzzed from the continued contact with the tiny bundles of energy, lightening her heart and her step, giving her the sense she could take on the world.

Anything was possible.

She just had to decide where to focus her potential.

Nick?

She blinked.

No.

Home.

Olivia bit her lip.

The buzz faded.

If he wouldn't let her just leave, Olivia would help Nick and his folks prepare for the big night, first. The world's children were far more important than any of her worries.

She smiled as excitement shivered through her.

I've never been part of something so important before!

Then she would figure out how to get home, and deal with her own problems.

How?

The memory of the blackened, wispy creature that had chased them shuddered through her, dragging her smile away. The oily shadow that had overlaid Mr. Anderson's features in the nightmare she'd woken from that morning.

From out of nowhere, Nick had appeared, to stop Mr. Anderson from hurting her—from possibly killing her.

Now, with time alone to think, the memories played out and the shock finally began to settle in.

He nearly did kill me.

Still, the acceptance that Mr. Anderson would willingly do something so drastic remained slippery.

If Nick hadn't...

Were both events truly connected? Nick seemed to think so. He'd said that Mr. Anderson had smelled of sulfur, like the creature had.

Olivia hadn't noticed, surrounded by the garbage bins, and then she was suddenly defending herself from his unexpected attack.

But why had he attacked her?

Olivia had been trying to help him find work for weeks.

Someone had told him that she was the cause of his distress. Who and why?

She sighed, rubbing her shaking hands over her face as she struggled to recount everything that had happened in the last twenty-four hours.

They'd gone back inside to serve dinner to the locals that needed it, as though nothing had happened. Because, what else could she have done? Constable Greer had come and taken Mr. Anderson away.

Had he learned anything from him? Had Mr. Anderson told him why he'd resorted to violence?

And the shadows.

I hope his daughter is alright. Will she be alright? Was sending him away the right thing to do?

She blew out a breath, pushing the hair off her face as she inhaled slowly.

Gena. Would she know what this thing was, and why it suddenly appeared out of nowhere?

Thoughts shifting, she released the breath, rolling the tension from her shoulders, and decided against involving Gena. Why would she know anything? Besides, Olivia had no desire to distress Gena, especially when she was doing so well, living among the humans these last few years. Well, mostly living among the humans—when Olivia coaxed her from her apartment to go shopping instead of ordering everything on line.

Gena was delicate. Nick wouldn't understand.

How could he?

Few knew of Gena's existence, which was how she preferred it. Even now, centuries later, she still lived looking over her shoulder.

No. Olivia would not bring her problems to Gena.

I'll figure this out on my own.

She dropped her head back, looking up at the sky.

Besides, if Nick's theory is true, whoever came after me was trying to get to Nick. Once Christmas night is passed and the seeds delivered, they should lose interest in me.

She swallowed a sigh, starting at the sound of wood on wood, turning in time to see Nick placing cut logs and his ax into the cart.

"We'll head back for lunch now." He slid his arms into the sleeves of his shirt.

Her gaze swept his glistening torso before turning away to give the twinkling overhead lights a last consideration before joining him. "It's so peaceful here."

Nick grasped the cart's handle, pulling it toward the forest path.

Singing drifted through the trees, the tune one that Olivia hadn't heard in centuries.

A wide smile stretched Nick's lips. He glanced at Olivia. "That'll be Dash, coming to usher us back before lunch is ruined."

A towering man with a shock of russet hair appeared as each party approached from around the trees, holding an impressive note in his song. As soon as he released it, he grinned at Nick.

"I know, I know, the spices are in a delicate state of balance and must be consumed before the optimal time leaves them withered and unappreciable."

Dash laughed, hearty and bold, shaking a thick finger at Nick. "Precisely. Now quit dawdling in the bushes with your lovely lady friend before you ruin her lunch."

Olivia couldn't suppress her giggle as Dash grasped her hand, bending to brush his lips over the back of her fingers. "Enchanted. You're hungry, yes? I see you are famished. Nick, you've worked her so hard she wilts like an exotic flower amid our weedy selves." Dash tsked at Nick, releasing Olivia's hand to snatch the cart handle from Nick. "Come. The others return with the Valkyries from the back lot. They have news."

"News?"

Dash grunted. "Yes, that's what I said. Food first, then news." He glanced back at Olivia. "If your lady can't keep up, you must toss her on your back. The whole thing will be congealing by now, Nicholas."

Nick's assessing gaze landed on Olivia.

"You're not seriously considering that?" she gaped at him.

"Why not?" he shrugged, reaching for her hand, he bent so that she could climb on his back.

"I'm not going to ride you, Nick!" Olivia's laugh turned into a squeal as Dash's paws gripped her hips to hoist her onto Nick's back.

"Him or me, somehow I think you prefer him." Dash gave her a little pat on the back once he was certain she wouldn't slide off, then went back for the cart handle and took off.

"Jésus, he's fast for such a large man!" From over Nick's shoulder, Olivia watched Dash speed away, then screamed as Nick launched into motion.

"He's just getting a head start." Nick sped past with Olivia's arms locked in a death grip around his shoulders and throat.

Dash's rich laugh floated in the distance behind them. "I know you can not resist a race, Nicholas! Lunch will be saved."

Bouncing on Nick's back, Olivia laughed, "you're lunatics!"

Soon, they breached the forest edge where a small crowd waited for their emergence, laughing at the sight of Olivia clinging to Nick's back like a stunned tarsier. She slid off the second he stopped, straightened her clothing and brushed the wind-tussled hair from her eyes.

"Praunci bet her dessert that you wouldn't do it." Vixen smiled up at Nick.

Nick shrugged. "Dash insisted I'd ruin Olivia's lunch if I didn't."

Vixen rolled her eyes, but winked up at Olivia as Dash emerged from the tree line with the cart in tow.

"He also said there was news."

"Aye, best come inside and settle down," Cupid held the hall's massive door open for everyone to file inside, now that Dash had arrived and rolled the cart into place alongside the others.

Chapter Seventeen

Blixem took it upon himself to introduce Olivia to everyone else. It was a challenge to memorize which Valkyrie's names—Praunci, Comyt and Dansa—were attached to the correct faces as everyone filed past; washing up, handing out dishes and passing around food platters.

They were an assortment of beings that Olivia had only heard of in heroic myths, or read about in books.

They seemed to crowd around her, though they'd all settled into their seats, asking her questions about life in Ottawa, craving information about the world outside of their own.

"Let her eat. You keep her talking so much she can't taste her food." Dash growled at his companions, most of whom rolled their eyes or chuckled, but turned to their own dishes.

The chicken on Olivia's plate was so tender and juicy she nearly groaned when the perfect blend of herbs and spices hit her tongue. She chewed, allowing the flavours to linger before swallowing. "My goodness, this is the best chicken I've ever tried."

Dash beamed. "Of course it is."

"You'll have ruined all other chicken for me."

He waved his fork in the air. "Inconsequential, since you're living here now."

"Oh, I'll be going home in a few days. As soon as Sleipnir is able to take me back."

"Nicholas?" Dash's head whipped in Nick's direction with a shocked gasp. "You can't return a gift such as this one."

Everyone's gaze swiveled to Nick.

"I—," Olivia started

"You said there was news." Nick's tone cut the discussion short before it turned into rounds of argument where everyone at the table no doubt would weigh in.

"There's a new anomaly forming." Praunci drank from her cup. "We're not sure how long its been there, but it isn't quite static like the one in the tower. It's in the cave with the underground spring."

"Sometimes it's there, sometimes not." Dansa added.

"Is it passable?"

Praunci shrugged. "We haven't seen evidence of anything coming or going through it. But we haven't been there consistently since one of the Nisse directed us to it. We had to focus on the harvest."

Nick nodded. "You put runes in place?"

"Of course. Though without knowing exactly what it is, it's difficult to ascertain which are best to use."

"This may have to do with the Ascension." Comyt added, setting her plate on the table before taking a seat, now that everyone else had their food.

"What is this Ascension that you've mentioned before?" Olivia set her fork aside, ignoring Dash's disappointed glance at the uneaten portions on her plate.

"O'Clery said it was a change in the balance between positive and negative forces." He drained his cup. "I don't know much more, though Ayo mentioned something about it when he cast us here. That we would be needed."

One Valkyrie cleared her throat. "From our lore, the Ascension is a time when our sun is moving toward her sister, bringing the cosmos closer together. As they draw near, the heavens will open, giving access to the other world."

"What happens then?" Olivia shivered.

The Valkyrie shrugged. "The stories aren't clear, as they blend together from different cycles. But magic and power is amplified."

"Sounds like Ragnarök." Donder grunted.

"Or Nirvana," Dansa countered.

"Neither of which are a balance. O'Clery's message from her sister was to stay the course. To keep the balance as long as possible?" Nick mused as his gaze met Olivia's. "Keep doing our job to maintain the balance. And protect the grove. Stay the course."

"The shadows?" her voice was soft, her heart growing heavy.

The shadows were someone's attempt to disrupt that balance somehow?

He nodded.

She swallowed trying to understand with this new perspective. "But if what you say about Mr. Anderson is right, he cornered me before you arrived to stop him. I don't understand how this fits in."

"O'Clery sent me in your direction—in her vague way."

"Her prediction had said I was in danger."

Love and danger.

Olivia dropped her gaze from Nick's, her to her fingers twisting on her lap.

Love.

"Could someone have seen you together?" Comyt asked.

"Before the attack in the alley, the only time we were together was at the party and the drive to Olivia's apartment the next morning."

"Sounds to me like O'Clery's got a leak." Dolph drained his cup, then refilled it.

Olivia started, not having noticed his presence at the far end of the room, apart from everyone else.

"I can't see how. Her place is heavily warded." Nick said.

"A tail then." Praunci dug into her food.

"That makes sense."

"Mr. Anderson served in the military." Olivia met Nick's gaze again, her stomach churning.

"Reconnaissance?"

"I believe so. Whatever happened during his service impacted his mental health. It's why he's having such difficulty since his return home. He hasn't been able to reintegrate with society."

Nick's eyes flicked to Dolph before dropping to his plate. After a moment he drew a deep breath. "Cupid, I need to get in contact with O'Clery's sister. We need more information."

Cupid nodded. "I've already requested a meeting. She's still in the field with her team, on a case." Cupid pulled back his sleeve to reveal a leather bracer with a metal device attached to it. "Vixen finished the modification this morning. I'll know as soon as someone reaches out to us."

Dash leaned across the table toward Olivia, whispering loud enough for all to hear. "There is pie."

Olivia smiled as the tension released from her stomach. "I love pie."

Dash grinned back. "Of course you do."

Nick jerked awake. Incessant pounding on the front door drew him from the chair he'd been sleeping on.

"Nick?"

Olivia appeared at his bedroom door, rubbing at her sleepy face, dressed only in one of his borrowed shirts, looking for all the world like she'd been made love to all night.

He dry-swallowed, tamping down the rush of desire already taking up residence between his thighs due to the vivid dreams he'd been enjoying before the abrupt disruption.

Dreams wherein Olivia had drifted, exactly as she was now, out to join him on the living room chair and—

"I'm coming!" Nick snarled at the door, wrenching it open to find a breathless Cupid scowling up at him.

"Took ye long enough." He held up his forearm to show him the surging rune on the bracer. "Ye got a call."

Nick spun away from the door, reaching for his boots.

"I'm coming with you," Olivia said hopping into her jeans at the threshold of the bedroom, socks gripped in her fist. Bluish discolouration lingered under her tired eyes. She didn't look any more rested than she had the previous day.

"Go," Nick said to Cupid. "We're coming." He tossed Olivia her coat as she slipped her feet into her boots.

After dessert the previous night, she'd made it very clear that if she was to stay, she was going to be a full member of the community until she could go home. And this business with the shadows was also her business, since it involved her community back home. Mr. Anderson. She was determined to figure out how to help him, if she could.

Nick had argued that maybe he couldn't be helped and she'd balked at that, scolding him for his lack of interest in even trying.

As far as Nick was concerned, he had more important things to worry about. Like the Grove's safety, and distributing the seeds.

And Olivia's well-being.

He didn't concern himself with helping men who attacked vulnerable women, even if one was potentially under the influence of a negative entity. In his experience, negative entities usually attached themselves to people who had something within them that allowed it.

Nick halted his thoughts from trailing on to his brother.

Centuries ago. Focus on the here and now.

Besides, Olivia's police Constable Greer took Anderson away. Problem solved.

They followed Cupid up the tower stairs to his communications room.

"You've certainly been busy in here," Nick commented, on seeing the array of equipment set up since the last time he'd been in the tower. The station resembled a security feed that he'd seen in the hotel, with multiple monitors, though created without a scrap of anything electronic. It was all made of raw minerals.

"I told ye Vixen and I have been working on some projects." Cupid grumbled, as he touched several panels of glowing crystals with runes etched into them, set below highly polished metal mirrors overlaid with sheets of the same cut crystal.

"Wow," Olivia breathed, taking in Cupid's workspace from her position by the door. "This is incredible."

"Aye. Glad you think so." Cupid grinned as his hands moved over the rune stones. "Ah, here we are."

Individual faces sharpened into view on three separate polished mirrors. "Quinn. Martin. While always nice to see you, its unfortunate to need to do so again so soon." Nick turned to the third panel. "I've not had the pleasure."

"Jolena Kane." The dark-haired woman offered.

"Joey is my sister, Nick." Quinn said.

"The one with the message for the Council." Martin supplied.

Nick nodded. "Of course."

"Cupid said you had a couple of incidents after I saw you." Quinn's voice was heavy with concern. "You were able to find Olivia?"

"He did." Olivia stepped to Nick's side, making herself visible to the callers. "And just in time too. He stopped Mr. Anderson from—well—his stopped him from doing anything foolish."

Quinn's brows rose. "Thank the Creator for that."

"And you think this is connected to our concerns?" Joey Kane looked thoughtful.

Nick recounted the details of both unusual events.

"And you're certain this entity was a threat?"

Olivia bristled at Ms. Kane's caution. "It certainly felt threatening, and I'm not one to jump at shadows, in general."

"The timing does seem questionable, but we can't automatically assume this threat is anything to do with us. It may just be something pursuing Ms. Boncoeur." Martin looked from Nick to Olivia.

"I did consider that, but given her lifestyle, it's highly doubtful—especially considering the timing. No, my instincts tell me this is directly connected. My people found another fissure that didn't exist before—at least one that wasn't detectable to us."

"Another fissure?" Joey pressed.

"We're communicating through one. This tower is built around it and it has been contained and controlled for centuries."

"You need to secure the new one immediately. Before it's discovered and infiltrated."

"We're already working on it, Ms. Kane." Cupid assured her. "My Vixen is already designing a portal containment, similar to the like of this one, based on the dimensions our folks provided, but with some added improvements. She should be done in a day or two."

"And we all need to hope a day or two from now isn't too late." Her gaze flicked to Nick.

"They're doing what they can, Joey." Quinn tried to ease her sister's alarm.

Joey frowned. "The Consortium is not to be treated lightly. They've already discovered the locations of a few portals. They'll be looking to control every one they can. We don't know how they're finding them yet, but we've been busy stopping them from gaining access."

"I understand," Nick assured her. "Your recent mission?"

Joey's lips compressed but she nodded.

"And everything is connected to this Ascension that Quinn told us about at the council meeting?" Martin cleared his throat.

"It is, at least on the subject of the inter-realm portals. I don't know about these shadows you've mentioned," Joey confirmed. "I'll pass along the details of your recent events and have one of my agents follow up with your Constable Greer and Mr. Anderson in Ottawa. It's imperative that you focus on distributing the harvest. I will be accessible at all times." Joey held up a crystal glowing on her palm.

"I'll—," Martin's words were cut short as the panels darkened.

A black film floated across their reflections in the polished sheets.

"What in the hells is that?" Cupid swore, pulling more runes up onto the ledge, whispering activation commands to push out the interference.

"Shut the frequency down."

"It won't do," Cupid growled.

"Olivia," a low, distorted, angry voice groaned through the room.

Nick grabbed more runes to combat the infiltration, adding tracking magic, in an effort to ascertain the source while they worked to push it out.

"Olivia!" The voice boomed, as the black film hijacked the frequency.

"What's happening?" Olivia gasped.

"I can't deactivate my rune," Quinn struggled to clear the magic to cut the connection.

"Nor can I," Martin backed away from his device.

Joey also backed away, speaking into her cell as she moved to troubleshoot her side. "Try to track where it's coming from."

Cupid and Nick moved as quickly as they could to rout whatever was happening.

A face began to form in the black mist, extending from the panels toward Olivia.

The second the being lifted several inches from the panel, Nick's hand shot out to freeze it before it could reach Olivia. With a fluid motion, he shoved her behind him, then pushed Cupid away from it.

Panting, Olivia peered from behind Nick's arm. "Jésus!"

Chapter Eighteen

Gena Black sat on the floor of her small apartment, facing the gold lamp set on the coffee table before her. Her fingers curled with the effort to hold the scrying spell she cast against the polished side of the gold vessel that harnessed her magic.

Olivia.

Since the moment she felt Olivia's absence from her auric field, she'd gone into a panic.

For two days she'd done all she could to find her closest friend. Her only family.

Olivia hadn't answered her phone, despite the numerous calls and messages.

Gena had gone to Liv's apartment, finding it abandoned as though she'd just gone out for the day.

So many worries bombarded her, ramping up her anxiety, till breathing was a struggle with the urge to vomit.

Despite her aversion to go out into public spaces, she'd done so after studying Olivia's planner.

Sunday she was due to work at the soup kitchen. Often Olivia would normally call Gena to check in on her and share updates as she ran her bath for the evening.

Gena spoke to Molly at the soup kitchen, who relayed what had happened with this Anderson human, then suggested she speak to Constable Graham Greer with the local police.

Her anger over these actions, and fear for Olivia's safety, overrode concerns over her own need to remain hidden from the world.

I have to find her, she repeated to herself.

And now, after two days of speaking to strangers and working spells to track Olivia's whereabouts, which had led her to a hotel rooftop, Gena feared the worst.

But there'd been no body discovered beyond the ledge. She'd apported herself up there to investigate for herself. The trail just ... ended. Mid-air.

Someone had taken her.

This Nicholas person that she'd left the community kitchen with.

Gena couldn't make sense of the mix of magical signatures on the rooftop.

Fear elevated to rage, unable to trace the one person that was more important to her eternal life than anyone else.

With a deep, deep breath to control the surge of emotion—as Olivia had taught her—she went home to think.

Now, after hours of focusing her limited power to find her friend, sweat beaded on her forehead and her fingers ached as she finally found the tiniest of gaps that suddenly opened, reconnecting Olivia's energy to hers.

She nearly cried as relief flooded her.

"Olivia!" She groaned, struggling to hold the magic.

Gena would not let that hook go and doubled down to push her power through the fissure to reach Olivia through the open frequency to a realm beyond the earthly one.

With a burst of glittering black smoke, she shoved her essence along the frequency, trying to reach Olivia.

If she could just touch her, it might be enough to pull her to safety from her captors.

"Olivia!" She screamed at the image reflected in the side of her golden lamp, allowing her rage and fear to ripple through the connection.

Her magic halted, frozen in place.

Who is strong enough to stop my power?

A tall blond man stood between Gena's mist and Olivia, blocking them from each other. He fit the description the humans had given her.

A shorter, bearded man—a dwarf shoved an activated rune toward Gena's mist trying to entrap her.

A resurgence of fear ripped through her.

No!

"Gena?" Olivia's voice floated through the connection. "Gena, is that you?"

"Stop it from getting in, you must protect the grove!" A female voice intruded along the open fissure connecting the access points to Olivia's location.

"Wait, Nick, stop! It's Gena. She's terrified. I can feel her fear." Olivia's voice broke through. "Gena, it's okay—I'm okay."

The second the hold on Gena's magic broke, she shoved forward again.

The blond man's hand jerked to stop her, but Olivia's hand grasped his, stopping him. "Nick, no. It's Gena."

"Who is this Gena?" the other female voice demanded.

"She's my friend. She's a Djinn." Olivia shouted. "Nick, please."

At his nod, all attempts to stop Gena from filtering along the power frequency ceased, allowing her to flow through enough, gathering her particles into a vague mass.

Olivia reached for her.

Gena enveloped her with her black mist, reassuring herself that Olivia was indeed whole and safe. At least for the moment.

"Your power, Gena, don't drain yourself." Olivia pleaded.

Retracting her particles, she demanded "Where the fuck are you, Olivia?"

Dolph eased up the tower steps on silent feet, mindful of any creaks in the worn wood, fists clenching and unclenching as his heart thumped in his ears. The pressure within him expanded, the closer he moved to the portal.

If he was close to the fissure, the connection he sought strengthened when Cupid opened the frequency. When he locked it closed, the connection was little more than an underlying hum in his system.

He closed his eyes, seeking that sliver of awareness.

Where are you? There's another portal, but it will take time to reach it.

Are you there?

The shouts tumbling down the stairwell froze him in place.

Have we been discovered? Has it started already? I told her to wait.

Too soon.

At the landing, he held his breath, listening, ever listening.

That was all he seemed to do any more.

She promised.

Fear rippled through Dolph's chest.

It could be a lie.

Worth the risk.

How much longer?

Gena? Who is Gena?

Not her. But who, then?

Dolph leaned around the thick beam supporting the roof, licking his dry lips.

He blinked, trying to make sense of the scene.

Three polished mirrors reflected individuals looking on as Cupid, Nick and his human spoke to a glittering black cloud writhing in the center of the room.

Another?

But he'd never seen it like this.

His pulse galloped.

Another!

This one made Dolph's black mist seem lesser than. Incomplete.

He strained to hear their exchange.

"Your power, Gena, don't drain yourself." Olivia pleaded.

Retracting her particles, she demanded "Where the fuck are you, Olivia?"

"Don't tell it anything. It's a trickster," Cupid growled, still struggling to figure out how to close the fissure and break the being's access.

"No, she isn't. Gena is my friend."

"Djinn don't have friends."

Olivia spun toward Cupid. "That's a mean thing to say, and yes, they do. It's Gena's magic that has granted me such a long life."

"Olivia, come home." The black mist extended a limb.

Olivia's hand rose to meet it, fingers extended.

"She can't, there's something trying to hurt her. That's why she's here."

"Anderson?"

"And something like you—some black entity tried to touch her."

"It felt wrong and smelled of sulfur."

"Olivia, I can't hold this portal open much longer." Its voice grew thin as the mist began to recoil into the polished mirrors. "My wards will protect you—," the misty limb lunged, wrapping itself around Olivia's wrist.

"No," Nick intervened, his magic colliding with the entity's as he grabbed Olivia's other arm.

Something popped and the mist exploded into the room.

Olivia screamed, reaching for it.

The pressure within Dolph surged, stealing his breath away for a few seconds.

The being spilled into the room, tumbling to the floor, forming into the ghostly shadow of a woman on her hands and knees. "What have you done? I can't exist here." She snarled up at Nick.

Dolph watched with excited interest.

Could this one get me out of here?

'You would betray our agreement?' the familiar voice finally loomed in his mind.

'No, I thought you abandoned me, not answering my call.'

'You answer my *summons, Alfar.'*

'Look.'

Dolph leaned so that the entity could see what he saw. The group in communication, and the new arrival.

'Leave! Before she senses us.' The voice boomed through his consciousness, causing his very bones to vibrate as the command sent him rushing down the stairs, losing some of its power the further from the portal he moved.

'I can't hear what's going on.' Dolph protested.

'If she discovers us, it could ruin all our efforts while she is attached to that human.'

'No, there's another portal opening, but it's much further away.'

'You said yourself there wasn't much time left, get rid of her. Breaking their connection will eliminate both of them as threats to our mission.'

Dolph's chest rose and fell. *'Kill her?'*

'If you want out of that place, uphold your end of the plan. We need access to those seeds and the timing is imperative. The seeds for your freedom.'

'You're sure your magic will work?' Dolph pressed as he darted a glance around to ensure he wasn't observed leaving the tower.

'You can stay there for eternity.'

Or oblivion. Worth the risk.

'I'll find a way to get you through.' He rushed along the path lining Cupid and Vixen's cottage as he made his way back to the hall.

The connection faded, though it remained a steady hum, digging at his consciousness.

He clenched his fists against the overwhelming need for a drink to settle the growing chaos within him. It quieted the ever-present noise.

"If those little fucking Nisse haven't drained every last drop."

Nick stared at the shadowy woman gripping Olivia's hand, unable to believe this was a Djinn.

After a lengthy discussion with the Fate sisters and the Council head—once he'd convinced Cupid to calm himself—they'd exchanged as much information as cautiously possible under the new circumstances. Cupid had shut everything down, warded the portal and they had regrouped at his place.

For the entirety of his long, long life, he'd always believed that the Djinn were on par with the Gods.

This creature held no resemblance to that belief.

He also reminded himself what the world believed himself to be. And he was not that either.

He passed Olivia a mug of warm cider from Vixen's tray, who'd kept her distance despite her deep need to be hospitable to guests. He ignored her thin lipped, disapproving glare.

"Hey, this is all your doing," he reminded her. "You and Cupid conspired and this is the results of your interference."

"We didn't expect your mate to come attached." Vixen snapped, jerking the empty serving tray away.

"We're not 'attached'. We're friends." Olivia's voice remained level, even though she'd said as much many times since Gena's unorthodox arrival.

"Well, technically, we are." Gena looked down at their hands. "A thread of my magic runs through you, maintaining our... friendship."

"You mean my life. Yes, well, that's different. You're not some entity whispering in my ear, telling me what to do."

The Djinn smiled. "No. You've always done as you pleased—what you think is right, regardless of my warnings."

Olivia rolled her eyes. "You make it sound as though I'm always getting into trouble, Gena."

Gena's answer was a shrug and a very pointed look around at their surroundings.

"This doesn't count—oh, you know what I mean," Olivia huffed.

"Nick, I don't like this. We can't regulate her."

Gena turned to Cupid. "While your system is a sound one, you never know if any of those other four in your frequency could have infiltrated something else."

"Four? No, we had three people in that call that you crashed."

"There were four energy signatures in that feed." Gena insisted. "Three female and one male."

"That's not possible." Cupid growled.

"And yet, I got through due to my connection with Olivia, once you opened the frequency. I couldn't find her before that." Gena's misty face turned to Olivia. "I can't stay here, Olivia.

Neither of us belong here. You need to come back. I need to get back before I'm lost. And you too."

"But you're Djinn." Olivia objected. "Your power is immense. Well, except for the whole lamp binding your powers thing. Is it because of that?"

"In part, yes, but as powerful as Djinn are, we are also limited to our world, where my power originates. As I said, I can only be here at all because of our connection. By all rights, you should not be here either, Olivia. We both need to go back."

"I will return her once we ensure her safety. We need to deal with this shadow threat."

"We need to deliver the harvest first," Cupid reminded everyone, as though they'd forgotten. "This is just a distraction."

"It is," Gena agreed. "Let me take Olivia home. My apartment is warded—,"

"Wait, go back to the bit where you said there were four in that call aside from yourself," Vixen pressed. "Not three."

Gena nodded. "Faint but definite. And brief. It came in right before I was ejected into this realm and disappeared shortly after. I was so focused on Olivia that I barely paid attention to it, let alone the others there."

Nick pinched his lip in thought, pulse ticking. "Dolph suggested maybe Quinn had a leak, that's how they found Olivia."

Cupid shook his head. "They had runes to enable direct access to the frequency."

"With the portal frame, there needs to be some direct connection to ride the frequency." Vixen said. "Like the runes."

"Or Gena's connection to me." Olivia turned worried eyes to Nick.

"So someone else had a rune or a connection of their own."

"But how? Sleipnir and I are the only ones that come and go." Nick's gut churned, as his thoughts turned to his brother.

No.

"And the Nisse."

Nick grunted. "Well yes, but they wouldn't allow infiltration. Their magic is very specific to them."

"But what if there is no portal container? Like that new one that opened? Can anyone come through it?"

Vixen nodded. "If the frequency and coordinates are discovered."

"Is there someone here that would do that?" Olivia's gaze flicked from Nick to Cupid and Vixen who pinned their attention on Nick.

Nick rolled his shoulders, shaking his head.

"Nick." Vixen's voice was unyielding.

"No."

"Nick." Cupid straightened his spine, "There is only one who has ever been miserable of this place. The one that caused us to be here in the first place."

"Not after all this time." Nick didn't meet their eyes. He couldn't, no matter that the thoughts had occurred to him.

I can't lay the blame of everything that goes wrong at his feet.

"Dolph hasn't changed, Nick." Vixen insisted.

"Not in all this time." Cupid added. "And he still can't touch the seeds. That says enough, doesn't it?"

"He can't?" Olivia's voice pulled Nick's gaze to her lovely face. "But he helps with the work here?"

He shook his head. "The only one here that can't."

"They shrivel and blacken." Vixen said. "He works on other things. Tending dead wood, building and repairing the cottages. Everything else."

"That doesn't mean he's the one—,"

"Who else, Nick? I told you he's been lurking about the tower."

Nick glared at the snap of Cupid's voice.

Vixen rubbed a hand on Nick's arm, voice soft. "He's ever been your weakness."

"Test it." Gena said. "Open the frequency, and I'll try to track the connection."

"I don't know that we should be trusting ye, either." Cupid scowled.

"You went to a lot of trouble to get me here and insisted I stay here with Nick." Olivia said.

Cupid nodded. "Aye, and?"

"Trust me?"

Cupid chewed over his thoughts but finally nodded again. "It were the fates that brought ye to us."

"Good, then you'll let us help figure this out. There isn't much time before Christmas Eve."

Chapter Nineteen

Olivia scanned the faces at the breakfast table in the great hall. Fatigue dragged at her as she lifted a cup to her lips.

Dolph was absent, as he had been all the previous day, since Gena's arrival.

The others had been casting surreptitious glances at Gena's misty form; a mixture of curiosity and suspicion.

"We haven't had so much excitement since we arrived here." Donder grumbled, sitting next to Olivia.

"None," Blix sat on her other side, mindful of Gena's swirling particles. "We've never had a Djinn serve the grove before."

"She can't stay." Olivia said.

"Neither can you," Gena was quick to add.

"Pity," Blix reached for a slice of warm bread. "Though I'm curious as to how you're able to be here at all. You're still fully living?"

Olivia shrugged with a chuckle. "As far as I know, yes. Maybe because I don't know the rules?" She blinked as the question slithered through her, as she met his serious gaze. "Wait, what do you mean by 'fully living'?"

"Olivia, this place is a part of the afterlife." Gena whispered. "A place for the dead to do whatever they do here, before moving on to their next phase."

Olivia stared at Gena's incorporeal face, then slowly looked at the rest of the individuals at the table. "They're all...?"

Gena nodded.

Olivia dropped her hands to her lap, twisting her fingers as questions and suspicions flooded her mind. "Am I?"

"Not yet."

Olivia searched Gena's face, unable to read her expression in her current state. "But?"

"It's best left forgotten, Liv. It was so long ago."

"Gena."

Her shoulders seemed to droop. "You were sick when your family left you at the dragon's cave."

Olivia nodded. "I remember. They thought I was going to die anyway, once the dragon came back to accept my sacrifice. But he never did. He just let me be. Took pity on me."

"He did. Then you found me, hidden away, and we became secret friends when he wasn't around, which was often. Your illness progressed, and I'd grown to love you as a sister."

Olivia's heart swelled with emotion as Gena's glittering onyx particles drifted over her entwined fingers still on her lap.

"You breathed your last breath and I couldn't stand the silence that followed. I'd been alone in that lamp for so long. And you—you brightened everything."

"I don't remember any of this." Olivia said.

"You were unconscious a long time."

"So why didn't you just cure her illness?" Donder shoved a chunk of ham into his mouth, reminding Olivia that they weren't alone.

Her gaze darted to the rest of the diners, regarding her with curiosity now.

"As a human, she was meant to have a finite life. I let her go—until she was gone and I—I couldn't stand it."

"So you brought me back from death?"

"I did. Your spirit still hovered nearby. It didn't take much to lure you back." She lifted an incorporeal shoulder. "We carried on as though you'd just had a rest. And, some time later, you hatched your plot to free me of my lamp."

Olivia huffed. "And failed."

"Not entirely. It was enough. And I loved you all the more for it."

"And gave me the gift of longevity." Olivia leaned into Gena's misty form.

"By then, I had realized that I shouldn't keep you with me. You couldn't live as you were in the dragon's cave, and had much to do in the world. You shone with it. It's what makes you special, Liv."

"And why you need to go back," Nick's voice cut in from the open door, cutting into their reminiscences. "But only once we make it safe for you."

The intensity of his gaze bore into her as her mind whirled.

What of Nick? Was he..? But he left this place. How else could he have been in Ottawa to meet her?

Blix leaned into Olivia's side. "Nick's different. More like you than us."

"He isn't Djinn-touched." Gena said.

Blix shook his head. "Something else, though I don't know what. Just who. I was already afloat by the time whatever happened, happened."

"Who?"

"Ayo." Donder said.

Olivia shook her head. "I don't know who that is."

"I've heard the name. He's one of the original 'Saints.'" Gena said.

"I forgot Nick was a saint." Olivia picked up her mug of warm cider with both hands.

"I'm not," Nick said from behind her, making her jump, splashing the cider on the table. "Cupid's ready for the transmission."

"Transmission?" Donder twisted around as Olivia rose from her seat.

Nick nodded. "We need to confirm final coordinates before we go. The Council is establishing a new point of contact for the hand-over of the requested extra barrels for the Nisse."

Don nodded, wiping his mouth and hands on a cotton napkin. "I'll let the others know, in case there is a change with the process and collection."

"There shouldn't be, but yes, we need to be prepared."

Olivia and Gena followed Nick out of the great hall. Just outside the door, they stopped.

"Ready?" Gena asked Olivia. To Nick she said, "Merging with Olivia's life force will mutually augment our power through our connection."

Olivia nodded with a deep breath.

Gena's glittering particles swirled around Olivia, tickling her skin as she surrounded her and slowly merged into her.

"Oh, this feels so weird," she whispered as the pressure of Gena's life force merged with her own from within her body, no longer a tether following her through the village. She felt as though they vied for space, awkwardly settling around one another without pushing the other out.

'Agreed.' Gena's voice sounded in Olivia's head.

Even with Gena's power as faded as it was, she trembled as it coursed through Olivia's human veins, heightening her senses.

It was a refreshing boost, after her lagging energy since her arrival. Like being at a different altitude, her body struggled to adjust.

Once Olivia had a handle on the new sensation of Gena riding within her, she followed Nick to the tower.

Curiously, she sensed the Nisse hiding in the bushes with watchful eyes like little glowing beacons of power, ones that felt different from Gena.

Her gaze swept the nearby forest, which now appeared wholly different than it had with her purely human eyes.

She gasped, transfixed, as currents became visible coursing up and down the trees, their branches radiating to the sky's light and deep down into the ground where their roots entwined. The vast network pumped energy down and around and back up with pulsing breaths.

"Nick, it's so beautiful," she breathed.

He stopped on the path midway to the tower, glancing between Olivia's face and the tree line.

The purest sense of interconnectivity bloomed within her, even though she stood apart from it. To see it, raw and pure, overwhelmed her.

"Do you see it, Nick? Is it always like this?" She swallowed, tears blurring her vision.

He studied the wide-eyed rapture on her face. "I don't think I do see what you're seeing, but I suppose it is." Turning to Olivia he scanned the hamlet and spoke at a slightly elevated volume, but not overtly obviously. "I'm going to take you with me to do the run, Olivia. When Sleipnir opens the portal, he'll hold it open while the crew bring in the barrels of ale and maple syrup as quickly as possible before we go. Once done, you and I will see to these shadows that targeted you."

"Maple syrup?" She blinked, finally turning her attention to Nick's face. The brilliant inner vision of the trees faded as she focused on his lovely face where his soul shone with a golden light. She blinked again trying to control her vision.

"The Nisse got the idea, hearing that you came from Canada and that I'd be taking you back at some point."

Olivia shook her head, unable to help smiling.

A shadow moved among the trees surrounding the hamlet.

'He's here. I can feel him.' Gena's voice was soft in Olivia's head. 'Wait here a moment so I can get better sense of him.'

Olivia reached for Nick's large hand. "I wanted to thank you for trying to keep me safe, Nick. Even though my presence has complicated things here. I—I just want you to know that I'm going to miss you." She searched his face.

While she was giving Gena time to do what she needed from within, she wanted to take the moment to say what she needed to Nick before it was lost in the whirlwind of later.

She stood on tiptoe, to kiss his cheek as she held his hand.

His warm fingers grasped hers as she eased away. He turned his face toward hers as though he was going to kiss her back. They both froze in place for a long moment, hovering close together. "I'm going to miss you too, Liv."

His breath was warm on her lips, sweet with cider as she met him, pressing her lips to his. His free hand rose, fingertips gentle on her face.

Her heart ached, swelling in her chest.

I love you.

The thought fluttered through her mind as she eased away from him.

The tip of his nose brushed against hers as he released her from his light grasp. "I wish..." he swallowed. "Let's go."

She nodded, closing her eyes against the surge of regret. Loss. Hers and his.

'Oh, Liv. I'm so sorry honey. We'll figure out a way to make this work somehow.' Gena soothed.

Olivia shook her head, blinking away the emotion gathering in her eyes. *'No. Forget it, it's done. Focus.'*

'My power is diminished here, but I can try to pull you through their communication portal with me. My apartment is warded and we can figure things out from there.' Gena reasoned.

Olivia smiled. *'As much as I love hanging out at your place, I actually would like to stay here a little longer.'*

'Nick?'

Olivia's heart sped up. *'And who can resist a night with Santa Claus on Christmas eve?'* Her breath hitched. *'The seeds—the trees are so special.'*

As they reached the base of the tower, Olivia's nape prickled. The draw of something heavy and dark pulled at her. The taint of something unnatural, resonating with a dissonance, intermingled with rich anger and bitterness.

'You feel that?' Gena's voice was strained against Olivia's consciousness as she trembled from within.

"He's coming," she whispered to Nick as they ascended.

"Dolph?"

"Yes, I think so."

The sensation of Nick's guilt washed over her. "Cupid's waiting."

'I don't like how this feels, Olivia. This Alfar is, or is influenced by, something dark and powerful, but I can't quite figure out what it is yet. Once the channel opens and I reconnect with our world, my power will increase and I'm going to do all I can to make things safe for your return.'

'I don't want you involved, Gena. I won't risk that bastard finding you, you've come too far to jeopardize your own peace and safety.'

'My past is the past. If he hasn't found me yet, perhaps he never will?'

They rarely discussed the individual, Gena's first love so very long ago, that had caused Gena's entrapment, and Olivia wouldn't press the issue further.

They stepped into the tower room where Cupid waited for their arrival.

'Do not put yourself at risk for me, Gena.'

Olivia gasped as the portal roiled with untapped electricity, contained within Vixen's crafted framework to control its access. The draw on Gena was significant, pulling at her particles, forcing her to work harder to remain attached to Olivia.

"One last Council meeting to finalize delivery details coming up." Cupid piped at Nick's signal, his hands fluttered over runes as he watched the polished panel.

With Gena's energy fused with her own, everything was heightened. She felt Cupid's aura. Felt the runes ignite as her vision caught their flare. Saw the thread of magic reaching for the framework that contained the portal fissure.

The portal opened with a blast of light that didn't seem to faze Nick or Cupid, reminding her of Sleipnir's portal.

Too many things were happening at once for her to focus on just one as Gena's power amplified her senses. Her gaze locked on Nick's incredible golden aura, calming herself as she allowed the sensations to wash over her.

Dolph slowly drew closer; his lower frequency made her gut churn, as she struggled to regulate her breathing.

'Ohhh...' Gena moaned, her anguish ripping through Olivia's body.

"No." Olivia gasped, unable to consciously grasp what was happening.

'Shattered,' Gena's voice trembled in Olivia's head as Gena struggled to maintain her connection to Olivia as her particles reached into the portal's connection.

The second the Councilman appeared on the panel creating an open connection, Gena locked onto both ends.

Her struggle ripped through Olivia, whose knees gave out. Nick caught her before she hit the floor. His grasp on her steadied her and gave Gena the grip she needed.

Dimly, Cupid's voice droned on as he spoke to the Councilman.

It—whatever it was—and Dolph, were just outside the door.

Impressions of power, and images, and energy signatures rippled through Olivia, overwhelming her body, as she was unable to filter any of it.

Finally Gena growled her revulsion. *'It's Djinn magic, Olivia. Shattered Djinn magic, being manipulated by someone in our world.'*

Through the storm of crackling magic, electricity and auras, Olivia sensed what Gena had found.

The entity was similar to Gena's own particles, but dissonant. Wrong. Then there was the female being that she'd mentioned before, whispering to Dolph through the connection. The domination of her will rode the black magic anchored within him.

Words were garbled. Her control of the magic was strong.

'Liv, stay close to Nick.' Gena gasped as she let go, flowing out of Olivia and back into the portal channel.

The room dimmed as Olivia's senses returned to normal. Her head spun as she leaned against Nick. "She's gone."

The portal crackled behind the panels, drawing Olivia's attention. Gena's sooty particles collected into a mass behind the Councilman, solidifying for a moment, lifting her hand before she faded into her glittering mist and drifted away again.

Nick and Olivia occupied the chairs of his living room in silence.

Her eyes remained fixed on the cooling cup of cider, her thumb tracing the imperfections in the rim of the glazed ceramic.

She hadn't said a word since her announcement that Gena had left.

He'd held her trembling body close, trying to ease her distress.

She seemed weaker than before the merge, amplifying his concerns that she was feeling the same effects that he did when he stayed away from the grove too long.

Nick focused on his own cup as impatience bunched his muscles, but he resisted the need to ask her anything until she was ready.

He could not imagine the intensity of a Djinn bond and therefore forced himself to be patient until she collected her thoughts to tell him what had happened.

All he knew was that Dolph had followed them. Nothing more.

It could mean anything. Nothing. Everything.

Finally, she sighed, set the cup aside and ran her palms down her thighs. "That was a lot."

He nodded looking into her haunted gaze as she searched to put her thoughts into words. "I can only imagine."

"She said..." Olivia bit her lip. "She said that there was shattered Djinn magic connected to Dolph that was being manipulated from someone in our world."

"How is that possible?" Nick stood, moving the cups to the dry sink, no longer able to contain the need to move—to act. "The third female presence?"

Olivia nodded. "I believe so."

Nick rubbed his hands over his face.

Dolph. Again.

After so very long here, and no change.

Perhaps this entity prevented it?

Perhaps this entity attached to Dolph was the cause of it?

Dolph had always had an edge to him, deeper than any other Alfar he'd ever known, but that night, the one that led to their thousand years tending the groves, had been his tipping point.

Everyone's tipping point.

"Ayo predicted this," he whispered.

Nick's heart twisted as he studied Olivia's lovely face strained with worry.

What role does she have to play in all of this?

"Did he?"

"In a sense, yes." Nick blew out his breath, pacing from chair to kitchen table and back. "My memory isn't clear on what happened—all I remember is that he said we'd be needed to keep the grove safe."

"But what do we do?"

"I don't know. Dolph isn't here to harm the groves, he's had centuries to do that." Nick rubbed his hands over his face. "For a long time, he seemed to be settling, changing. Calmer. But in the last century he started becoming edgy again."

Nick resumed pacing the limited space. "I have to call everyone. Cupid will already be working on the runes to pick up any more foreign traces. Vixen is headed for the other portal to finish securing it—if it can be done in time."

"Do you think whatever's going to happen will be soon?"

"I don't know. But we have to be prepared, whether it's tomorrow or ten years from now."

Chapter Twenty

CHRISTMAS EVE.

The Associate paced the wide bank of windows lining her office.

The winter streets were snow-strewn, streetlights decorated with red, white and green for the festive season.

And she hated it all.

This exaggerated cheeriness added to fuel her desire to crush it out of the folks that tried to 'do good' in the spirit of the season.

Bullshit.

She turned away, strolling past her desk, allowing her fingertip to brush the solid brass desk plate bearing her name, E. S. Chernalog, on her way to the decanters in the corner of the room.

Susan poured herself a glass of brandy, cradling it in her grasp as she approached the blueish glow of her laptop, admiring the crisp numbers of her report.

Her goal had been to downsize before the end of the quarter, and she'd successfully cut the company's costs in her allotted time. Her day job.

Seeing the devastation on the faces of the severed employees had given her the deepest thrill of power she'd ever tasted—aside from her control over the *Taints*.

That was wholly different, and special.

Though she liked it better when she could use the words 'you're fired', which no one used anymore, rather than 'let go' or 'laid off indefinitely'.

The best was last week, when she'd stood before that annoying Boncoeur woman and told her she was long longer needed.

Her expression had been priceless.

Her work had been good, exceptional even. Enough to warrant claiming it as Susan's own and giving the company executives excuses to allow her to end Boncoeur's contract.

Who could have guessed she would have to deal with her again? That she would get herself tangled up in Susan's mission to disrupt her target's ability to do his job? That was vital for tilting the balance.

Nicholas Klaus.

Her off-the-clock job. Her true work. The day job was more of a hobby that paid her condo expenses and provided cheap thrills.

Susan scowled, disgusted with her sloppy work. Olivia had evaded her efforts to get rid of her, disappearing into the other realm. The coveted one.

The one that held the true currency of the world. What reality was built on.

The whimsy of hopes, dreams and wishes. Raw potential.

No matter. The pawn will take care of it, now that they were assured the second djinn had left the realm, clearing the way for their work to continue.

The waiting would soon be over.

Everyone was in place, now that she'd got her pawn on track. The spore had gone dormant after so long in the otherworld, but she'd nurtured it back to action; her hook to control him, and do the Consortium's bidding.

After years of infiltrating his dreams, studying his desires, growing the connection, she had him.

Dolph wanted out of that realm. It was a simple promise to make.

It probably would happen at some point, anyway, not that Susan herself had any control over that.

Tipping the glass to her lips, she sipped the liquor.

Some point. Probably long after she no longer had any concern with him or it, and was firmly on the Consortium's board, overseeing the next phase of the Ascension.

A grin stretched her lips and she sighed, contented.

Returning the glass to the decanter tray, she glanced at the uncovered mirror.

I should check in.

She'd given the pawn his instructions. The Consortium's team were in place.

Susan glanced at her watch, moving toward the scrying mirror she kept in her workspace. A simple make-up mirror, spelled to tap into the Taints' power.

She smiled, sliding her fingers over the locket that held the processed djinn shard.

The Taints.

Susan never could have imagined that she would be entrusted to handle such powerful magic as fractured djinn power, created and harvested centuries ago.

But she had earned the Consortium's trust. Done exquisite work to prove herself, and was committed to continue doing so.

She was never told how they came to possess such rare magic. Just that they did, and they accepted her as part of the team dedicated to handle the Taints and their corresponding spores.

Pure corruption.

She shivered, savouring the sensation of knowing it was in her grasp.

So close.

She removed the locket, words of power on her lips, preparing to open the channels as she stared into the mirror.

Chapter Twenty-One

Olivia brought the last of her baskets to the cart.

Sweat beaded on her forehead as she gripped the edge of the cart to catch her breath, body trembling. Each day she awoke feeling weaker.

Still, she was determined to be of service while she was in this realm.

They'd set out to work in the last pocket of the grove needing care.

All day everyone worked until Sleipnir decided it was time.

On alert, they were also watchful for Dolph's return. No one knew where he'd disappeared to and she could no longer sense his presence, as she and Gena had together.

Not knowing his location kept her on edge.

What will he do? Anything?

All day her thoughts bounced between worries over Dolph and heartache over Nick.

These last days with him felt like none she'd ever experienced in her life.

And yet he made it clear she didn't belong here.

The weakness in her body confirmed it.

But her heart didn't hurt any less.

Nick belonged here.

She belonged in her lonely Ottawa apartment, job searching and spending Sunday nights on the phone with Gena while she had her bath.

Olivia loved her best friend, and Gena needed her.

But the ache persisted. Her heart beat Nick's name.

Drawing a deep breath, she returned her thoughts to the king of horses.

The Portal Master.

Sleipnir was the key, the one to determine the absolute timing.

Olivia was determined to set aside her fear of the great magical warhorse, with his wicked hooves and intimidating teeth. He was her only way home, now that she'd sent Gena back through the communication portal.

He could still bite or crush me...

I could call Gena back... somehow?

She dismissed the thought and returned her attention to the cart.

There weren't any other baskets, and nothing else to gather seedlings into.

Extracting a flask of water, she turned, listening for the thud of Nick's ax, then started toward the direction of the sound.

She found him working at the base of an ancient oak, surrounded by a vast ring of saplings. The Aurora Borealis was strong above the saplings, a wall of light in the sky around the grove, anchored to the bright seeds filling their lush branches. Despite its thinned crown, the oak still stood, testament to its sacredness, filling her with awe.

Loath to disturb his steady pace, she settled on one of the fallen logs, content to watch unnoticed.

His skin glistened under the rainbow of brilliant light as he drew the ax up and dropped it with the full power of his body, splitting the remnants of dead branches. Over and over again, Nick worked ceaselessly, lost in his rhythm. He'd tied his long pale hair up off his neck, though several tendrils clung to his moist shoulders.

Olivia licked her lips as the sight of his bunching muscles reminded her of their bed play. Her gaze traveled down his back to the perfection of his behind. The heat of his body made his pants cling to the encased muscles, clearly defining every inch of him.

She crossed her legs as her body reacted, making her as slick as he was and pulsing with the need to have him fill her. Clenching her fists, she crossed her arms, resting her elbows on her knee to lock herself in place, lest she approach him.

Swoosh, thump. Swoosh, thump. Swoosh, thump.

His arms arced over head as he brought the ax down, splitting the wood to tumble down to the waiting pile. Placing a new log, he kept going.

Olivia didn't know how long she watched, but the need didn't abate. It fueled her memories and fantasies for new encounters that she knew would never happen.

With nothing else to do but wait, she allowed it, soaking up the sight of him while she could.

She squirmed on the log, unwilling to give up these moments, no matter how uncomfortable her body became, wanting all of the visions of him seared into her memory as possible.

Finally, when the last dropped bough had been split, Nick straightened, face turned to the sky eyes closed, ax loose in his grasp as he caught his breath.

Olivia shot to her feet, flask in hand, approaching before she realized she was moving.

Before him, her eyes drank in the sweating sight, his skin flushed, muscles taut.

She whispered his name.

Turning his face down to hers as he opened his eyes, she held the flask up for him.

He took it, chest still rising and falling with his efforts and drank deep of the cool water.

Her full attention fell to his throat as he drank.

When Nick held out the flask, his dark eyes sparked as he read her face.

Her nipples pebbled under this assessing gaze.

She made no effort to hide her desire for him.

"Olivia, I—," he sighed.

"I can't stay away, Nick." Her fingertips smoothed over his hand holding the flask, taking it from him.

The contact seemed to be enough as he growled, reaching for her. "I can't either, Liv. You're all I can think about." His hand slid around her nape, pulling her closer as his lips descended over hers.

She moaned into his mouth, pressing herself to him as he arched around her. He was hard against her belly, so very hard, inciting her to rub against him.

As much as she wanted this, she hadn't expected it.

If he wanted to touch her, she'd take all she could get.

Nick dropped the ax, freeing his hand to grasp her bottom, crushing her to him. The flask fell beside it.

She panted as she slid her hand into the front his pants to grasp and stroke his hard length.

He groaned, breaking the kiss, leaning his forehead against hers as she worked him. "Liv." He warned, voice tight.

"Nick, I need you." The words worked their way up from her core, squeezed her heart and tumbled from her lips, reverberating back through her chest.

More than just desire.

I need you.

She'd never *needed* anyone before.

But the longing for him tore through her.

When they parted, she'd never be the same.

She already wasn't.

"Now."

Before our time runs out...

Consuming her mouth, he backed her up to the Oak's trunk, mindful of the massive, upturned roots. When she did stumble, he caught her, pulled her up into his arms so that she could wrap her legs around his slim hips. The second her back hit the rough bark, his hips pinned her in place, his hard length pressed to her moist heat through their pants, rocking against her, inciting sparks of pleasure.

Her hands roamed over his back and down to his bottom, squeezing as his lips and teeth grazed the sensitive flesh of her throat. His hands slid up her sides, taking her shirt up until he cupped her breasts.

Liv couldn't get close enough, though there wasn't a speck of wasted space between them. She shoved at his pants, frustrated by the belt and button.

Growling, she dropped her feet so that she could rid herself of this problem, then tore at her own. Nick pulled her shirt up over her head and she made quick work of her bra.

They stood, panting, drinking in one another's naked bodies dappled in the magical light reflected from above.

He was long and hard and ready, a pearl glistened on his tip.

Her need renewed in a flood, setting her flesh afire as she looked up into his face. His desire, his attention, was focused on her. He didn't speak, but the emotions were clear in his eyes.

This is it.

They both knew it.

Her heart pounded in her chest, she was hot and ready, their urgency just under the surface.

Yet, here, now, the moment suddenly felt as sacred as the oak itself, opening their hearts.

They were about to consummate what was in their hearts, though neither breathed a word of it.

This would be all, forever, once they parted ways.

She back to her life among the mortals, and he tending his duties here in this nether realm.

Their one night a year, could not be. It would destroy them both.

You don't belong here...

She wasn't one of them, whatever that meant in this place.

This time with him was a gift and she would accept it and cherish it with every fiber of her existence.

Attraction brought them together, magic made it meaningful.

This knowledge was reflected in his eyes.

There was no doubt that he cared for her as his fingers traced the contours of her face, memorizing. With both hands cupping her cheeks he leaned, touching his lips to hers.

Olivia's heart twisted with the utter tenderness in how he reached for her.

Her hands retraced their journey along his ribs and back. She leaned into the tree, gently pulling Nick closer, renewing the contact.

Need pulsed through both of them, her right hand slid between their bodies, grasping and stroking his rigid length until he nipped her chin.

Guiding him to her entrance, she claimed his lips.

She cried out as he filled her to her sweet spot. Pinned to the tree, her muscles clenched around him so hard she took his breath away. Unable to stop herself, she moved against him, weakening his control and inciting him to thrust.

Resting her head against the tree as he worked in and out of her, she opened her eyes to its crown above.

The lights overhead glowed brighter.

She blinked, surely it was just her?

But it wasn't. The ring of trees surrounding the grove dazzled the entire space.

The magic.

The magic was cresting. The seeds in the trees blazed under the wavering magic dust in the sky.

Olivia could barely think for the rising haze taking over her body. "Nick, look." She panted, knowing that he needed to see it too.

He searched her face, then looked up without stopping, he couldn't, the drive had taken over as she clung to him.

Everything fell away as he realized what was happening over head. The raw emotion in his expression when he looked at Olivia ripped her heart open, sending her over the edge, dragging him with her.

Every pin prick of light surged along with them.

Nick's strained whisper drew her attention. "I've just found you. I can't stay away from you, I don't know how I'm going to let you go, Liv." Bracing himself with one hand on the trunk by her head, with his free hand he gently lifted one of hers from his shoulders, kissed her fingers and placed her palm over his heart. "I can't keep you."

"I know." She leaned up to kiss his lip. "We have right now."

"It isn't enough."

"It has to be."

He drew her to him, carefully laying her down on the mossy ground at a junction between two of the oak's massive roots. The ground was soft and spongy beneath them as they continued to explore one another's bodies, while admiring the fluctuating light dance overhead.

They made love again before they dressed, collected the results of their day's work and headed back to Nick's hamlet.

Dolph crept among the shadows, following the human through the woods as she collected the seeds, singing and talking to herself as she went.

She was comely. As comely has Hedi had been, though she lacked the warrior's ferocity that Hedi had possessed.

It was easy to see why Nick was interested in this one. It was easy to see how he could forget Hedi and let go of her memory.

Hedi had chosen Nick over Dolph; why, he'd never understand. He'd concluded that it was because she didn't fully appreciate the Alfar qualities that Nick lacked, preferring Nick's pasty hue to Dolph's rich indigo. But Dolph had been the one to remain steadfast, during her life—and her death.

Dolph had been the one to declare absolute vengeance to honor her and her children with Nick.

Not Nick.

He refused to complete the task of annihilating their enemies. And had stopped Dolph from doing it as well.

Nick never deserved Hedi.

And he was the reason they were all trapped here. Not enjoying the afterlife in Valhalla, or even returning for a new lifetime.

Because of *his* guilt.

Because he hadn't honored Hedi and their children as he should have.

Because he had stopped Dolph from doing the task and the children of their enemy have since thrived, even though their own people withered.

Dolph was sure of it. He was sure it was Nick's shortcomings as a warrior and leader that plucked them from that battlefield and dropped them into this place, like flies in amber coalescing around them.

But at least, here, Dolph could still hamper Nick's work.

The veil was thinning. The festering ooze that filled his heart whispered the time was coming.

Then he could act, redeem himself for failing to properly avenge Hedi and punish Nick for it. For every wrong Nick had ever flung at Dolph. For existing when he should never have been created by their mother and that human she'd taken to her bed.

For bringing Hedi into their family and then making her reject Dolph for Nick.

And for imprisoning them in this desolate place full of the trees they tended and the unending stream of light in the darkened sky. No sun, no moon, nothing more.

Dolph remained to the shadows as Olivia approached Nick, chopping the deadwood.

He observed as she watched Nick, hungrily squirming. He'd barely finished when she'd leapt to her feet, offering water.

Had they even exchanged any words before they were pawing at each other?

The way she looked at him, with clinging hands and needy eyes, sent daggers of jealousy ripping through Dolph.

Anger ripped through him. Disgust rent him as he continued to watch, unable to turn away as Nick backed the human woman up against the tree and fucked her.

Unable to resist, as he watched, imagining he was the one burying himself in her body. He'd have worked her much harder and faster, regardless if she enjoyed it or not. He couldn't decide which would be better.

She wasn't Hedi, but he couldn't help casting Hedi's face on her—imagining himself inside of her.

That was what he'd wanted. Always. To claim her and use her as much as he enshrined her memory.

Even though, she too was a human.

Dolph loved her and hated her.

He couldn't tear his gaze away as he watched his half brother pump into her. They were almost there, he could hear her gasps and moans.

Then the sky brightened. They all paused, looking up.

The lights, the seeds that Dolph could never touch without killing them, the trees, the grove itself brightened, expanding with color so brilliant over the canopy of the oak that it hurt his sensitive Alfar eyes.

It seemed to react to their coupling.

They continued, with a slower, measured pace as they paid more attention to each other.

It was easier watching Cupid and Vixen. They didn't usually complicate things with the need to linger and caress. When they were in the woods, they just fucked. Like everyone else in this damned place.

But the magic never reacted to them like it did now.

Not even the Nisse, when they mated.

The human moaned. She was nearly there.

Nick brought her over the edge, going taut as he filled her.

The overhead lights surged, a gentle shower of glittering dust floated around the couple, panting against the tree.

Had they seen it? Had they noticed?

What did it mean? Anything?

He'd have to report this unexpected change in the grove and see if it affected the plan or not.

Then, he just needed to decide if he was going to destroy this watered-down version of Hedi that Nick had found to replace her with—as he'd been ordered to do.

Or keep her for himself?

For now, there was work to do.

Dolph had relayed the meeting point to his dark voiced wizard so she could fulfill her mission and grant Dolph his extraction from this place.

He'd already left a cluster of dead seeds, soaked in his blood, stuffed into the crevices of the cave where the new portal appeared. *She* had said it would strengthen the connection. Now he needed to do the same around the tower portal before Sleipnir and Nick opened theirs.

Excitement twisted through him.

It's almost time.

Chapter Twenty-Two

Nick lay on the mossy ground, holding a peaceful Olivia in his arms.

He gently brushed a lock of hair from her forehead as she slept. The overhead lights maintained their brilliance since their love making.

Love making.

Love.

How in all the heavens am I going to let her go?

He pressed his lips to her temple, gentle so as not to wake her, just yet.

He thought of the last few days and how right it felt to have her near, despite his efforts to keep his distance.

Everyone but Dolph had welcomed her, accepted her as one of them. Gathered around at mealtimes, they'd shared drinks and stories after working alongside one another all day.

Nick desperately wanted her to belong there with them. But it couldn't be.

Olivia already had a home—a life elsewhere. Her community needed her golden heart and bright smile.

Their bodies cooled, and she shivered against him.

Nick pulled her all the more to him, trailing his fingers down her glistening arm, dragging away a shining residue that he'd thought was from their exertions.

Rubbing it between his fingertips, he noticed it clung to her entire body, and his.

Finally he looked up through the oak's great crown to see the nearly imperceptible particles drifting over them like the finest pollen.

Olivia sighed in her sleep, inhaling deeply as she rolled toward him, nestling ever closer against his chest. Her eyes fluttered open to stare into his.

She smiled, reaching for him, tracing his brow as he'd done to her countless times while she slept.

The glittering dust clung to her lashes, cheeks, nose and lips. Her eyes—her beautiful blue eyes—reflected the colors above them.

"It's time."

The slightest crease marred the perfection of her brow, clearing in a heartbeat. She nodded with a tender smile. "I won't ever forget this moment, Nick."

His throat worked. "Nor will I." He searched her face. "I want you to know—you're so—," he blew out his breath searching for the right words.

There would be no time later. Not if they were to have the clean break that was needed to move on after tonight.

She placed a fingertip over his lips before he found what he was looking for. "No words." She pulled him down to kiss her with such sweetness, his heart ached.

I wish...

I can't...

There were no promises he could make. He didn't have that luxury.

This was it.

Instead of words, he put everything he felt into that kiss, deepening and prolonging it until they were both breathless.

When he finally released her, her eyes fluttered open a second time, glistening with emotion reflecting the brilliance around them.

The atmosphere enveloping the couple hummed with energy, making his skin crackle.

He'd never experienced anything like this before. Certainly not here, where everything remains unchanged.

Both dressed in silence, though they often cast one another glances. Once finished, Nick pulled Olivia into his arms one last time, crushing her to him. He hoped that she would understand.

Understand that he couldn't have her no matter how much he wanted her at his side, in his bed—his arms. Always.

She'd stolen his heart that quickly. Just a matter of days.

No. It was that first smile.

He swallowed as he released her.

He'd loved Hedi, and their children, with every bit of who he was.

This was different. A different kind of love.

Unless... but how?

"What is it?" Olivia reached out to touch him, eyes searching his face.

Although Cupid and Vixen had contrived to get Nick out to Quinn O'Clery's party, Quinn had accepted the task, and was pleased they'd met.

'Perfect! You're both here and you've met already...Damn, I'm good at this.'

Quinn was a Fate. She'd sent him off in Olivia's direction that night at the soup kitchen. Was it because she sensed danger? Or because she wanted Nick to meet Olivia again?

Both?

Was this why fate had brought them together? To remind him of what it was to live and love? To remember what it was like?

He swallowed, throat tight.

"Nothing." He shook the thoughts from his mind, smiled and kissed her forehead before slipping his fingers through hers. Collecting his ax, he led her back to the cart where the baskets of seeds waited for them. After pulling his shirt and coat back on, he carefully slung the basket strap over his shoulder, gripped the ax in one hand, and reclaimed Olivia's hand in the other for the return trip.

The snap of a twig drew Nick's attention to a distant cluster of trees.

He tensed, slowing his stride.

A shadow moved between them.

Dolph?

Probably a Nisse.

In all the time he'd been here, his warrior's instincts never faded, though there was never a reason to be on alert. Not here in this place of peace and magic.

Quinn's warnings slithered back into his mind, dragging up the distant memory of his meeting with Ayo.

'The Grove needs to be tended and protected at all times. Its value is immeasurable.'

'Stay the course.'

"Nick?" Olivia's soft voice drew his attention to her concerned face. "Something isn't right. I feel it."

"Let's get you back to Cupid's place. The others will be gathering soon. Blix and Don will be nearly finished funneling the crop into the satchels for tonight and will need these." He gestured to the brilliant seeds, resuming his pace, mind racing.

The shadowy creature from the alley reeked of sulfur and it hadn't made it close enough to touch either of them.

Did it need to? Was proximity enough?

He glanced down at Olivia as they moved. The man that had attacked her stank of it too. He'd touched her; could it have transferred something to her?

No.

The grove magic reacted to her, but not in the way that presumed something menacing or negative.

Like it did with Dolph, who never touched the seeds since their arrival, when they'd withered on contact. So long ago.

Contrary to Olivia's experience. It shone all the brighter.

Dolph?

No.

His brother stank, but not of sulfur. Rancid alcohol and unwashed body.

Enough to mask other odors?

No.

Nick's feet moved faster.

Vixen had said that Dolph was Nick's weakness.

Nick's jaw clenched as he guided Olivia back to the others.

Not now. Not after all this time.

'...we are leaning into the Ascension, and we're at a delicate tipping point between those driving the negative and positive forces.'

'My sister is working on the front lines to maintain the balance. Our job is to stay the course on the home front. It matters.'

Nick didn't slow his pace until the roof lines of their cottages came into view. "I'm not sure what's going on, but something isn't right. I want you to stay with Vixen while I figure things out."

Olivia gripped his hand. "No, I'll stay with you, Nick."

Startled, he looked down into her luminous eyes, where stardust seemed to have gathered, as she struggled to catch her breath. He blinked, observing the strange change and the intensity of her expression as she stared up into his eyes.

He nodded.

Nick gently unslung the basket as they approached Blix and Don's workstation in a clearing behind the cottages. Full baskets were neatly lined up, empty ones haphazardly tossed aside. Each carrying one of the magical leather satchels, they sped down the line, gently tipping seeds inside them. Their natural Alfar abilities allowing them to move with swift accuracy.

Blix glanced up without slowing. "Dash is prepping Sleipnir's gear."

"Cupid?"

"Tower."

"Dolph?"

Blix shrugged. "Haven't seen him."

Nick grunted, heading toward Vixen's smithy. Her eyes lit up when she saw Olivia enter with him. He hefted the ax and she nodded toward the work bench.

"We secured the new portal fissure early this morning." Vixen reported

Nick turned back, "Relieved to hear that report."

Olivia had moved toward the back of Vixen's shop, her attention focused on Nick's ancient weapon, affixed to the wall along with everyone else's.

He shivered as her fingers reached up to slide down its haft. "Olivia?"

"This one is yours. You should take it."

He and Vixen exchanged glances. How had she known that one was his?

"Everyone should." Olivia looked at the rest of the collection.

Vixen's eyes widened. "That's not creepy. What in all the hells, Nick?" She sucked in a breath when Olivia turned toward her. The colours in her eyes intensified. "Nick?"

"I dunno, Vix. Whatever is happening is just since I took her to the oak grove."

"The big one?"

He nodded.

"The spore is growing and seeks to let more in."

Ice slid down Nick's spine at Olivia's words. "Liv?"

"Protect the seeds."

"What does she mean?" Vixen demanded. "What spores? There's never been anything of the sort here."

"I'm not sure." Nick pulled the weapon down from the wall, reacquainting himself with the feel of its grip in his palms.

"Dolph? He's the only one that can't touch the seeds, and never has, since that first time they withered under his care. But he wouldn't—if he was going to harm the grove, he's had centuries to do it, if he'd ever intended to." She searched Nick's face. "He wouldn't. Someone, or thing else?"

Vixen removed her smithy apron.

"We don't have time for this, we have to get the work done while the window is optimal for Sleipnir." Nick growled.

"Nothing changed until her arrival. Maybe it's her, Nick."

Nick glanced at Olivia again. "You're not wrong, Vix. But look at her. The grove did something to her eyes. It's using her to communicate a warning. It wouldn't do that if she was the threat itself." Nick pulled several of the other weapons from the wall, handing a war hammer to Vixen. "This has to do with the Council meeting."

Vixen nodded, though she cast another sidelong glance at Olivia. "Best gather the others."

"We have to keep working as though nothing has changed, but be on guard for anything. I'm going to talk to Cupid. And then try to find Dolph."

"I'll talk to the others. Quietly."

Olivia saw everything through a misty rainbow film. No matter where she glanced, her eyes were coated with stardust.

Her skin sheened and tingled.

Since she'd awakened in Nick's arms under the tree, thoughts drifted into her mind. Thoughts in her own internal voice, but so random, they could only come from elsewhere.

And feelings. Like a little shuttle sliding up and down her body from crown to core.

Her nape registered being observed before they'd heard the twig snap.

The sensation of ill intent reached for her.

Her human sense felt as heightened as when she and Gena had shared her body.

Despite Nick's speed to return to the village, Olivia was bombarded with whirling thoughts and feelings from not just the trees around her, but the beings too. Their brief meeting with Blix and Don cast to her their focus, and determination to see their work done with precision and speed. Vixen's delight to see them return, and her concern over Olivia's words, even as Olivia herself seemed to take a backseat to their coming.

They flowed off her tongue like fact.

The grove sensed danger. A fungus threatened it in some way, that even it still sought Olivia's words to communicate.

She slipped out of the back door of Vixen's forge, compelled to move closer to the tree line.

Gena's magic had allowed Olivia to *see*.

The Grove's magic ripped open her empathy.

Emotions assaulted her from all sides as the grove's consciousness flowed along the power threads she'd seen before, carrying information from crown to root, exchanging and mingling far below the surface.

It knew.

The Grove had been watchful of the dark mote floating among its woods for all this time.

It was aware of the astral changes.

The trees had seen it all before.

It had nearly been wiped out during one cycle, thoroughly dominated in another and preferred not to have either repeated.

The grove had imparted all of this information by the time they'd reached Vixen's cottage.

An age was a long time to exist under a suppressive element.

Olivia sensed both portals, old and new, with a distant awareness and knew there would be more in the coming times. There always were. These two were as secure as they could be.

Sleipnir.

The Grove drove Olivia's sight through the forest back toward the clearing where she and Nick had their last moments together—where the atmosphere shimmered the most.

She saw it all now, with this new lens. This particular tree's roots stretched the deepest into the ground, its branches dominating the glittering sky.

Sleipnir stepped into the clearing, grazing below the outstretched boughs.

Olivia's breath caught as her vision wavered.

Her heart constricted as the figure of a woman was superimposed the tree trunk, when Sleipnir raised his head to look at her with a man's eyes.

Breath stalled in Olivia's chest as she dropped to her knees.

He truly was a king, and she his queen, living out their cycle, preparing to walk the realm at the pinnacle of the cycle, experiencing existence as human beings for the designated period of time.

Not yet, but soon.

But if the wrong forces dominated the groves, they would spend this next section of the cycle as prisoners, their seeds exploited.

Olivia experienced the thoughts through her emotions. As the magic soaked deeper into her skin, so too did the grove's connection.

Images of the past filtered through her mind, making her heart pound.

She blinked.

The mote of darkness drifted away, toward the writhing blaze of the communication tower in the distance.

She sucked in a breath, trying to absorb everything she'd been shown, startling when Sleipnir's hoof thumped the ground next to her.

Lost in the visions, she hadn't noticed his approach.

Drawn into the depths of his keen eyes, she swallowed.

It was time.

His power was at its peak, for Nicholas to do what was needed.

Chapter Twenty-Three

Apprehension rippled along Vixen's shoulders and down her spine.

The change in Nick's mate had been unsettling, but it was clear she'd somehow gained a connection to the grove's soul.

She understood now that this was why Cupid had been having the dreams that drove him to seek out the Fate who made soul connections.

It was time.

She wasn't just Nick's destiny, she was theirs too, though in what way, Vixen could not guess.

But knowing her Cupid had the biggest heart, it made sense that the grove would impose this necessary mission on him.

She didn't know how it would be possible for Olivia to stay among them, especially when she'd already started showing signs that her body wasn't compatible with this realm.

Vixen shivered, as possible scenarios flickered through her mind.

Shaking them off, she redirected her thoughts to the task at hand.

It was Vixen's job to ensure the warriors' weapons were ready to defend the realm, should the time of need be now.

They still could not know for sure, though Olivia's changes imparted a sense of urgency.

As soon as she'd secured the new portal fissure, Vixen had assigned a group of Valkyries to guard it.

She hoped they were enough to secure it against whatever Dolph was doing.

And she'd never had any doubt that Dolph would one day prove to be a blackguard and could not understand why Ayo had sent him here with the rest of them.

Vixen just prayed that what happened a thousand years ago would not be repeated.

It was unfair to Nick.

Her heart had broken for him, being put in a position of having to end his brother with his own sword.

It had been the only way to save the temple full of vulnerable children, hiding, with their solitary protector—an old, one-eyed man with nothing but a gnarled staff.

Nick had tried to reason with Dolph, that killing the innocent children would not honour their dead kin.

A contingent of their raiding crew had broken off, following Dolph's lead, laying waste to the village while Nick had focused on fighting the warriors defending it.

Raiding was their way.

And it hadn't ended well—for anyone.

Now, with a thousand years of existence in a place such as this grove, Vixen, and all the others, saw the folly of such a way of life.

⁎

Olivia watched as Nick tightened Sleipnir's riding gear, murmuring to the great beast, who kept his eyes trained on her.

She shivered as her eyes swept his massive runed hooves, sooty coat and neatly braided mane and tail.

Did Nick know? Did everyone here know? Is that why the thrones in the hall remained in place?

Perhaps there would be time to ask later. Perhaps not.

Nick was determined to help her solve the shadow creature problem as soon as they completed the seed delivery.

And how long would that take?

Maybe not so long, now that they'd had contact with Joey Kane who said she would have her agents look into the matter.

And then?

Nick would come back here to carry on the work, and I would do the same in my world.

She swallowed the lump of emotion rising from her throbbing heart.

Olivia lifted her trembling fingers. After the third day, she'd begun to weaken.

There'd been a brief boost of energy when the grove had fused its magic to her body, but it had dissipated after a few hours, leaving the emotional connection reduced to a steady hum.

She teared up. In these few days living and working alongside them, enveloped by their warm company, she'd begun to feel accepted. The same way she did with Gena.

Mixed emotions continued to swirl around her. Focus on the job, worry about the threat, curiosity over the outcome.

Several Nisse ran past her, toward the gathering, anticipating the arrival of their imported goods.

She glanced around the small clearing with a bittersweet smile as she adjusted her jacket and checked her pockets for her gloves.

Dolph was still no where to be seen as everyone else lingered, while Nick prepared for the journey.

I'll never see any of them again.

She rolled her shoulders. Like every other time she'd allowed herself to be immersed in a community—allowed herself to feel like she had family—something always jerked her right out of it.

This was no different.

She'd known from the start this was temporary, no matter Cupid's insistence that it was otherwise.

Nick mounted Sleipnir's back, settling into the saddle, slipping his feet into the stirrups.

Blix and Don held up the two satchels, carrying millions of colourful seeds in their depths. Nick slung a strap over each shoulder, settling the bulk against the opposing hip.

Vixen passed him his ax, which found its place across his back.

Pulling his leather gloves on, Nick's gaze found Olivia's, he held out a hand for her to join him.

She drew a deep breath, glancing at Sleipnir again. He emanated nothing but... resolution? And some impatience to be away and started on this crucial annual mission.

And she was somehow part of it. This one night. A gift.

With a breath, she stepped forward. Cupid appeared, blocking her path, eyes shining in the depths of his thick eyebrows and bearded face. "Ye'll be back, I know it." He gave her a curt nod and stepped away again.

There wouldn't be time for good-byes later, once the portal opened, the others would have to act fast to move the barrels into the carts. Nick and Olivia needed to be ready atop Sleipnir as soon as the task was done.

She smiled glancing at the others who wore grim or guarded expressions. "I hope so."

Olivia approached Nick, reaching for his hand to climb up into the saddle in front of him. She squealed when two massive paws gripped her hips, lifting her effortlessly to Nick's height.

Glancing backward, Dash's eyes twinkled up at her. "Remember my chicken."

"I will. And pie." She grinned back at him as he stepped away.

Sleipnir wasted no more time, moving toward the mountain ridge, with its underground corridor leading out into the barren snowscape beyond.

The rest of the crew followed, pulling the carts previously used to harvest seeds and collect dead fall. Now, they would bear the Nisse's beloved barrels of ale and much anticipated maple syrup. It was a fair exchange for their devotion to the groves.

Tension locked Nick's muscles as he trained his eyes and ears on their surroundings as they approached the entrance to the grove side of the mountain ridge. The weight of his ax heavy on his back, though familiar, even after all this time.

His arms tightened around Olivia without meaning to. Even though she leaned back into his chest, she was as tense as Nick was.

Seated as she was, her scent drifted up to Nick, drawing his gaze to her profile, committing both to memory. His chest ached as he resisted the need to tighten his grasp on her, to pull her closer and claim her lips. To keep her with him.

He would let her go. He had to.

She didn't talk or ask questions as she had on their arrival.

Within the mountain ridge, the multicolored torch light flickered to life, lighting their way.

The only sounds once they moved inside were the echoes of Sleipnir's hooves reverberating off the stone, followed by the distant rattle of carts, making it nearly impossible for his crew to talk without shouting over the racket.

That and the somber shroud of anticipation of what lay ahead.

Would they be betrayed? Again?

Sleipnir's ears were alert, his sides expanding as he scented the air while he carried them forward.

Where is Dolph?

He wasn't always part of the send off, but more often than not he was present if for nothing more than to alleviate his boredom.

Nick's heart clung to his brother's innocence.

Surely, he'd be here to help oversee the restocking of the ale barrels, especially since they'd run out already.

But this time, in light of the concern following Olivia and their suspicions, Nick remained uneasy.

Nick, you can't ignore what happened in the communications tower.

Though the information had come from Olivia and her djinn friend, Cupid had been able to confirm traces of the other energy signature.

The great doors to the outside winter wonderland loomed into view, sweeping open with great gusts of frigid air at their arrival.

Sleipnir carried them to the threshold.

"He's here." Olivia gasped as Sleipnir tensed. "All I can sense is his anger, Nick. His darkness is stronger than before."

Nick's gaze darted around the corridor, landing on the shadows to the side of the great doors where Olivia's attention lay.

His nape prickled, unable to see his brother in the loamy darkness.

Behind them, the line of carts trundled to a stop.

Sleipnir stopped with a huff as Dolph stepped out.

They had to go, there was no choice.

Nick's fingers tightened on the leather reins. "Dolph."

"I just came to ensure you took that human back where it belongs." Dolph's tight voice hissed along the stone, his lips curled, creating deep, dark ridges and valleys in his bluish face, giving him the appearance of the Krampus, the Scourge from the ancient stories.

"That's the intention."

"And you're still set to collect the ale?"

Nick nodded, watching his brother.

"Good, those little bastards hid the last barrel from me. I haven't had a drink in days."

Nick frowned. "They're entitled to it for all the work they do. It's fair payment."

Dolph's eyes narrowed on Nick, flicking to Olivia as he moved closer. "I don't ask for much. Never have."

Sleipnir grumbled, sidestepping away from the Alfar. Dolph persisted, reaching for the great horse's reins with one hand, running the other along his neck to the edge of the saddle where his hand slipped to Olivia's knee.

She shuddered at the touch, jerking her leg away from him as Sleipnir side-stepped again, pulling them away from Dolph's reaching hand.

Dolph held his hands up, backing away with a mirthless smirk as a fresh eddy of cold air swirled snow across the threshold, dragging the stink of unwashed male and sulfur across their faces.

"Back away from her!" Nick planted his foot on Dolph's chest, shoving him away from Olivia.

Sleipnir stomped a hoof.

They had to go.

He turned in the saddle, locking eyes with Vixen, and with the hand shielded from Dolph's view gave her the warning signal.

Lips compressed, she nodded, reaching into the cart.

Nick nudged Sleipnir's side with his knee.

Right there, at the threshold between the grove realm hidden in the mountain ridge and the winterscape of the north pole, the portal ignited with a pop as energy crackled around them, brightening the interior of the stone corridor.

Their last location on the hotel rooftop in Ottawa became visible through the ring of electricity, a blizzard raging there.

The crew slid around Sleipnir, eyes flicking warily toward Dolph. They'd pulled their weapons from the carts and fastened them to their bodies.

Nick nodded through the portal to the familiar face of their ale supplier, already rolling the barrels toward Sleipnir's position through the rigid, swirling snow to where Nick's family would receive and load them into the carts. He studied the faces of the others, not recognizing any of them.

Although Nick and his crew always came armed, this was the first time in centuries that they anticipated trouble.

Barrels through, Sleipnir drew breath, muscles bunched, to begin the run.

From the shadowy corner where Dolph waited, his lips stretched into a wide grin.

Nick lifted his hand, prepared to freeze anyone that might come near them.

As Sleipnir crossed the threshold between mountain stone and city rooftop, a shout sounded.

In an instant, black smoky chains whipped out from under the front edge of the saddle, encircled Sleipnir's body, and drove themselves into the ground, halting him mid stride. The portal's electricity snapped and writhed.

The force set Nick off balance, allowing Dolph to lunge forward, grasp his outstretched arm, and pull him to the ground.

Olivia screamed his name from atop Sleipnir, but part of the black chain trapped her leg, holding her in place.

A wave of black slithering shadows loomed up over the rooftop, flowing over snow drifts, rushing toward the open portal.

Nick continued to grapple with Dolph as his crew dispersed toward the torches lining the cavern walls, seeking to combat the shades.

"Should have held the status quo, and not tipped the balance, Nick." Dolph growled into Nick's face, adjusting his grip on Nick's shoulder, his forearm pressed to his throat, a knee crushed Nick's arms into the stone below them. "As long as you remained apathetic, they were content to leave this place alone — at least for now."

"Ayo warned me you wouldn't be content to tend the grove. He said you wanted too much." He panted through his compressed windpipe, struggling to see Olivia.

"I wanted vengeance Nick. Total. You always knew that. I was crystal clear. I never hid who I was."

"They were children, Dolph. Not our enemies. Their parents—and their elders—were more than enough to end things." With a twist of his body, he managed to shove Dolph off of him and turned to freeze the writhing shadows surrounding Olivia.

Dolph rolled to the side, pulling a wicked mace from the shadows where he'd been hiding.

Nick grabbed his ax, instead, as the stench of sulfur filled the cavern, riding the storm's bluster.

He spared Olivia a glance, struggling against one of the barrel men, who was trying to pull her from Sleipnir's back. Sleipnir bucked against the black magical chains, trying to free himself.

"It's never enough!" Dolph ran toward Nick, swinging. Several of the iron spikes grazed Nick's cheek as he turned away from the attack. "Humans are the ones who want too much." He swung again, but Nick was ready for it, swiping the mace head away with the head of his ax.

Nick parried another swing. "Stop this. What's wrong with you? We've tended these groves together for a millennium. Someone has spellbound your mind."

"No one has done anything to me. I've been holding my position. Quiet, patient. Vigilant for the day I would leave this fucking place."

Nick stepped back, absorbing this.

"You may have gaps in your memory, Nick. But I don't. I remember what happened. Clear as yesterday."

His gaze flicked to the man holding the wicked knife point to Olivia's delicate throat. Her eyes were wide over the hand covering her mouth.

Nick had accused her of trying to see the best in everyone.

For over a thousand years, he'd blinded himself with the exact same sentiment.

Nick had always known what Dolph was. He'd always seen it. He'd known.

He just couldn't face it.

His brother.

And he'd sentenced his whole crew along with him. For his failings.

For Dolph.

He'd never deserved it. He wasn't worthy of their sacrifice.

Nick wasn't worthy.

A fissure in Nick's mind slid open with a soft whisper.

A memory buried with a few of Ayo's words. It rose to the surface now, clearing the debris of so many other memories. The good, the bad, mostly the mundane.

An elusive pappus, always floating just beyond his grasp, drifted back to him.

If Nick hadn't agreed to the contract, they'd have all gone into netherworld together. Not this Other world, let alone Valhalla.

What he'd done.

Left so many dead in the wake of their tsunami of vengeance.

An endless cycle of retaliations.

Turned a blind eye to Dolph's true nature.

He glanced at Olivia again, past Dolph's prowling form.

No, he didn't deserve her.

She was the essence of what this place was supposed to be.

Light. Hope. Potential.

A gift to the world.

Not his to keep.

She would gladly do this work. She wanted to do it.

Nick couldn't give it to her. It was his mantle to bear.

But he now understood that he couldn't do it without her. Not the way it needed to be done.

Her human soul belonged in the mortal world. An immortal among mortals, quietly doling out mercy and grace wherever she went.

He craved that.

Nick craved Olivia's sweetness. She was never blind. She saw the evil as well as the good, and chose to act on the good.

He craved her grace, the glow of her soul.

And as much as he wanted to embrace her for himself, he was desperate to set her aside and cast her out to preserve that purity of heart.

For the world that needed it more than he did.

He needed her love to carry on, until the powers that be decided it was enough. Not him.

She needed to go. She couldn't survive in his world anyway, not without the final step and there was no way Nick was going to let that happen.

Nick pressed the edge of his ax to Dolph's neck.

Black mist swirled through the whites of Dolph's eyes.

A woman's chanting became audible from the rooftop as sleet blew in through Sleipnir's crackling portal.

With a glance at the approaching woman, whose hands were outstretched to control the writhing shadows, Dolph snarled through gritted teeth, straining against Nick's fury. "A thousand years of giving these children hope, Nick. Nearly destroyed me, and would have, were it not for the knowledge that it had purpose. To feed into the Ascension. Something to trade when the gates opened between the worlds." He gave a short laugh. "And we're nearly there. I will be able to walk in the world again."

"Our time there is long gone, Dolph."

"Yours hasn't been. Back and forth you go, every gods damned year while the rest of us are trapped among the trees. Because of you." Dolph growled when Nick blocked another swing. With the next, the brothers battled until Nick looped his ax around the mace head, ripping it from Dolph's grasp as he struck out with his other fist. Both weapons sailed through the air, skittering with a crash into the stone wall. Dolph recovered, drawing his dagger from its sheath as he advanced on Nick.

"Nick!" Olivia ran toward him. He glanced back to see Dash swinging at her captor as Sleipnir continued to buck against the restraints. The Nisse had appeared, struggling to free the warhorse from the bonds.

"I will go, Nick. I will no longer exist in this place!" Dolph lunged, seeking to sink the blade into Nick's shoulder.

"No!" Olivia screamed as the blade's tip punctured the flesh, and deflected off the collarbone. Nick's free hand jerked up, freezing everything as Olivia slid between the brothers, her palms on their chests to shove them away from each other.

Nick gasped a ragged breath as light filled the cavern, blinding him.

Chapter Twenty-Four

Olivia's heart pounded as she struggled against the black chain, pinning her to Sleipnir's saddle. Chaos exploded beyond the portal and flowed into the confines of the mountain corridor.

Taints—djinn shards, as Gena had called them—rose up over the edge of the icy rooftop, flowing toward them. Several surrounded the men working to deliver the barrels in a cloud of roiling, sulfuric masses, disappearing up into the men's nostrils and eye sockets.

Eyes blackened, the men turned toward Olivia; one passed a hand over the chain, releasing her from it while it remained to trap Sleipnir, as the man dragged her from the portal master's back, knife pinned to her throat.

Donder roared her name, but he was waylaid by two of the possessed men running toward him. It was enough to draw Dash's attention to her. In moments his great body descended on her captor, who shoved her aside to deal with this new threat.

Vixen spun into place, weapon raised to defend Olivia.

"Don't kill them, they're possessed!" she screamed over the din of clashing weapons and grunting combatants.

"Not very practical, Ms. Boncoeur. I will not release any of them from my spell now that I have them." A woman's voice snapped across the expanse.

Olivia spun around to face Ms. Chernalog, balanced on the rooftop ledge, the edges of her coat whipping in the fierce wind.

Gaping, she gasped, fists clenched. "Wha—You? Where did you come from?" But the woman ignored Olivia, her clawed hand outstretched, focused on Nick and Dolph, a thick black thread writhed toward the latter, intent on attacking his brother.

Unsure what to do to stop them, Olivia was moving before she'd completed the decision, running toward the two, fear strangling her. She ran past the Nisse trying to free Sleipnir, one stretched, reaching for her. Ignoring the weapons and powerful fists, she slid between the brothers, hands outstretched, intent on shoving them apart, with no other thought than to stop them from hurting each other.

Nick's hand lifted as Olivia felt tiny hands grasp her leg.

"No!" She screamed, slamming her palms against both Nick and Dolph. Light exploded in all direction then everything froze, blinding white.

Her breath whooshed in her ears as she stood, frozen in place, one hand on Nick's beating heart, the other on Dolph's. A Nisse clung to her leg, monkey-like, with one hand on Sleipnir.

Nothing but white space surrounded them, snow and sleet a twisted wall, cutting them off from everything else. The edges tinged with the colours of the aurora borealis, fizzling both around and within her.

Her connection to the grove was strong at this threshold between the other realm and her world, held open by Sleipnir's portal and with the power of the Nisse reinforcing her connection to it.

The grove's consciousness imparted information to her with each breath she drew.

Threads of power wove their way around each individual, even Dolph, though black smoke rose from a pinhole in his shoulder. Her vision flickered, showing her the black veins stretching inward toward his heart, eating away at the coloured threads circulating through his body.

Her heart ached, understanding how the grove's magic struggled within Dolph against the blackness.

The light brightened.

A scene exploded before her, like a movie playing out, less the confines of a screen.

Around them, the chaos of a destroyed village raged. Much like the current scene of battle, this one was just as visceral.

The stench of blood and smoke from burning cottages and bodies filled her nose and coated her tongue as she gasped for breath.

She'd seen the like before, in her long lifetime. This scene was not one of those.

It was much older, centuries before her birth.

An old man in grey robes ushered a troop of children toward a simple stone building, glancing back over his shoulder with one good eye. Carved statues and offerings were strewn across the threshold, knocked from their place when the invaders flooded the village.

Dolph came into view, leading a band of warriors, eyes fixed on the group of children seeking shelter in the temple.

Nick, engaged with a defender, glanced toward his brother. Seeing his intent, he quickly discharged the enemy and ran to block Dolph's progress.

From the edge of a hut, a dark figure loomed, unseen by everyone else, observing.

"No, Dolph. Let them be. We've done enough here."

"We promised to avenge our kin, Nicholas. Your wife. Your children. My kin. Our family." He lifted his sword.

Nick wavered, chest heaving from the fighting. "This is not the warrior's way. We don't slaughter children."

"They will grow, and come for what's left of ours if we don't."

"Perhaps not. This won't bring the lost back to us. If you do this, you will not see them in Valhalla, Dolph."

It was Dolph's turn to waver, the men behind him waiting for his command.

Finally Dolph nodded, and after a long moment, he lowered his sword.

By now, the rest of Nick's crew—his chosen family—surrounded him, facing Dolph and the other warriors who were intent on vengeance.

Olivia swallowed, feeling the heartache emanating from him. From both of them.

The dark figure lifted what appeared to be a blow dart to its obscured face.

Dolph jerked, his free hand swiped at his shoulder, knocking something to the ground.

Olivia saw it then. The smoky thread drifting from Dolph's shoulder back to the figure, who lifted their hands, twisting and curling.

Dolph's shoulders lifted, his sword came up between himself and Nick. Shadows flickered in his eyes as he glanced toward the temple. "Get out of my way, brother. I have work to finish here."

Olivia felt Nick's heart break as he stepped up to stop Dolph, resolved.

They battled, long and fierce.

Dolph, larger and stronger than Nick, backed him all the way to the temple door, eventually crashing through it.

He battered Nick relentlessly, on his way to dispatch the old man guarding the children.

Olivia couldn't move, helpless to do anything but watch and absorb every broken heartbeat.

It was all happening so fast.

The scent of sulfur mingled with the stench of chaos.

The warriors slaughtered each other. The last to fall outside the temple door was Cupid, taking down the warrior coming up on Vixen as she fell to a dagger in the back.

"Ye're brothers," he cried, bleeding on the step, Vixen's inert body in his arms. "Stop this!"

The black figure followed, chanting, thickening the smoke controlling Dolph as he tried to hack through Nick toward the old man shielding the children cowering in the corner.

Dolph disarmed Nick, sending his ax clattering to the stone floor of the temple.

Nick's hand shot out, freezing Dolph in place, as he wrenched the sword from his hand, in a bid to stop his advance.

Dolph unfroze, startled to have his sword taken from him, and he withdrew a dagger.

Nick froze him again.

The dark figure chanted louder, more insistent.

The old man guarding the children, trying to shield them from the vicious battle, screamed at the figure. "This will not gain you the access you want! You will not take the grove."

"We will have it." The figure sent a blast of black magic in the old man's direction. A shield of coloured light deflected it, blinding the attacker, forcing them back. "You're too weak to fight all of us at once, old man, *and* defend the humans."

Dolph advanced, lunging forward with a great arc to drive his dagger into him, giving Nick no choice. He lifted the sword, stopping Dolph's attack. Both fell to the ground.

The sword penetrated Dolph's chest, piercing his heart.

Nick gasped as blood flowed from an open wound, so profusely there was little hope of stopping it.

The old man stepped forward, hands raised against the black figure. With their dark champion no longer between them, the figure retreated from the broken temple door, disappearing into the shadows.

The old man got down on his knees, laying hands on Nick, murmuring next to his ear.

Olivia could not hear the words. She watched as tears flowed, in utter heartbreak.

It was the past, there was no changing it.

Finally, Nick nodded to whatever the old man had asked him.

He reached up, clasped the one-eyed man's hand and coughed.

In an instant the scene changed.

Nick, Dolph and the rest of the crew stood facing the grove, staring in awed confusion at the northern lights glimmering in the sky over the mountain entrance.

With a wave of the old man's hand, the great doors opened.

"What happened? Where are we?" Nick sputtered, eyes flicking to his equally confused family.

"I am Ayo, and I will explain along the way." He lead them inside. "We have great work to do. Great, important work to do."

They filed along behind him. Dolph was the last to go, but go he did.

On his shoulder a single black mote burrowed deeper into his shoulder.

Olivia gasped as the scene dropped away and they were again in the cavern, back in their current time, still ensnared in Nick's time freeze.

Magic rippled through her. Power fizzled from her heart to her palms, reminding her of Gena's particles, only instead of black djinn glitter, it was full of the aural colours of the borealis. The magic connecting sky to grove.

A little zap on her leg from the Nisse triggered the flow within her, pushing it toward her palms, still slammed against the battling brothers.

The squeezed her eyes shut, allowing her empathic connection to open as emotions flowed from one palm to another, channeling the pain and love and grief between Nick and Dolph.

The grove had tried to heal Dolph, but the single spore had lingered, digging deeper as the Ascension loomed ever closer, encircling his heart in the black infection, preventing him from healing. Without healing, Dolph could not move on.

Olivia, filled with the grove's power, boosted by the Nisse, and now able to tap into Gena's djinn particles as well, found she was able to focus on that single spore, created from a djinn shard, as healing magic flowed from her palms.

It eased through Nick, mingling with his natural golden glow, travelled through Olivia, and into Dolph's misty grey soul energy, until it pushed the blackened spore back through is own channels to the pinpoint in Dolph's shoulder.

It retreated, exiting the skin, tumbling to the ground like a pebble of lava rock.

At that point, all of the dark wisps of magic binding Sleipnir retracted with a snap toward the dark mage controlling the Taints from the rooftop.

The Nisse let go. Nick's power released its hold and Olivia collapsed into his arms.

Dolph dropped the dagger as he too fell to the ground, panting, wide-eyed, hand clutched to his chest as he stared from Olivia to Nick. "I—you..."

Olivia's breath hitched as Dolph's aura brightened.

Dolph's attention swung toward the battle that continued around them. Gaze dropping to the floor, he kicked the blackened pebble through the open portal and out of the mountain's corridor.

Olivia spared a glance, noting that Joey Kane and some of her agents had somehow arrived during the moment that they were locked in the netherworld spell, and were working to subdue the dark mage.

"Go! You have to deliver the seeds." Dolph nodded toward Sleipnir, who huffed as several Nisse clung to his mane, hissing at the Taints beyond the crackling portal.

Stumbling to his feet, Nick glanced back to Cupid and Vixen, on guard within the corridor, unable to engage outside the portal. Both nodded as they monitored the battle outside.

"I can't feel the spore here anymore." Olivia said as Nick helped her up.

He helped her up into the saddle, mounting behind her. Blix and Donder retrieved the cast-aside satchels, handing them back up to Nick, then backed away to fill the gap in the line of defense behind them.

"We'll sort things out here, don't waste any more time." Cupid shouted, waving for them to go.

Sleipnir danced on the spot, looking to regain his footing as his muscles bunched to into action after straining against the magical bonds for so long.

The Nisse squealed as he launched forward. Olivia held her breath as they raced toward the edge of the rooftop.

The mage turned toward them, hand raised.

Nick froze her in place, and the Nisse jumped from Sleipnir's back, dragging the frozen mage to the ground as Sleipnir raced past her over the side of the building.

Sleipnir's magic crackled as they soared through the air, making Olivia's stomach lurch.

The instant Sleipnir's hooves passed into the astral realm, he kept running, the charge of his magic encircling Nick, drawing their power together.

Olivia's stomach churned and her head swam as she remained in place atop the horse. Nick dismounted with a satchel. His image flickered, appearing and disappearing in one place to another so fast it all blurred together.

She struggled to hold onto her dinner as motion sickness threatened to overwhelm her.

Maybe I was a little hasty in offering to take over...

She swallowed, sucking in a breath, only to realize they seemed to be in another time zone, somewhere in the eastern part of the world.

Locked in Sleipnir's saddle, there was no sense of time as all things happened at once; though Sleipnir seemed to be running ceaselessly, they didn't move forward. The scenes flowed around them, blending from one to another.

At some point, Nick swapped out the satchels and carried on.

Finally, they reappeared on the hotel roof that they'd launched from, devoid of the corridor to the mountain which held Nick's beloved crew.

Joey Kane and her agents, as well as the dark mage who had weirdly turned out to be her former supervisor, Susan Chernalog, were all long gone. The blizzard had calmed to gently drifting snow.

Only Gena stood there, waiting next to the access door, eyes closed, her face bathed in the light of the sun cresting the horizon.

Sleipnir released his magic, cantering to a stop, his sides heaving.

Nick dismounted, then helped Olivia slide down to her feet. Her knees wobbled and backside ached.

Sleipnir huffed, shaking his head and body out, releasing the tension in his muscles.

Gena stepped forward, arms outstretched. "I sensed you come and go, so I thought I'd come and wait for you here. You left quite a scene in your wake."

"Oh?" Olivia gripped Gena tight.

"Agent Kane and her men arrested your old boss—what was her name—Chernalog? The fourth person in that meeting."

Olivia nodded.

"Interesting turn of events." Gena lifted a brow. "I put Kane in contact with your friend, Constable Greer. He's launching a local investigation into Chernalog's activities here for corporate corruption while Kane's group looks into the djinn shards. Seems they have ways to bind her magic, rendering her powerless to hurt anyone else." Her expression tightened.

"Mr. Anderson?"

Gena nodded. "I think he'll be alright, once Chernalog is stripped of her power over him." She turned to Nick. "And you brought my Olivia back to me. Thank you."

Olivia turned back to Nick.

His face was pale, devoid of expression, but Olivia felt the intense churn of emotions radiating from him. She reached out, brushing her hand over his, giving his fingers a light squeeze as she searched his eyes.

"I'm glad its safe for you to return home." He cleared his throat.

"I'll meet you downstairs, Liv." Gena went through the access door, leaving them alone.

"It's been one heck of a week," Olivia released a pent breath, brows raised.

"That it has."

Olivia's heart flipped.

This is it. Our time had run out. For real this time.

"Maybe I'll see you around." Olivia forced a smile as she committed his features to memory. "Find a nice atrium some-where—,"

Nick dipped his head, claiming her lips, crushing her to him with a rush of fierce need.

She instantly gave into him, arms gripping him equally as fierce, deepening the kiss, hoping it would never end.

But it would.

It had to.

This was it.

Olivia broke the kiss first, eyes closed.

Nick sighed, kissing her forehead.

She leaned her ear to his chest, listening to his heart thump before burying her nose into his shirt, inhaling his unique cinnamon scent.

"I'm going to miss you."

He sighed, voice tight. "I'm going to miss you too, my Livy."

She smiled, heart twisting.

Olivia let go, easing back out of his embrace. "Tell everyone I—I'll miss them too. You have a great family, Nick. *Great* family."

"I'm glad you think so." He lifted a hand, stroking her cheek, then let it fall away. "You take care of Gena."

"Always."

Olivia turned toward Sleipnir.

He watched her approach with unblinking eyes.

"Nick's right. You are magnificent."

Sleipnir huffed, pressing his head into her shoulder, allowing her to feel his delight and reciprocated sentiment.

She ran a hand along his neck, marveling in his silky strength. "King and Portal Master," she whispered. "I am honoured."

She turned for one last look at Nick, standing alone, eyes glued to her face with such intensity it drew her to him.

She looked up into his dark eyes, feeling all the longevity, the stoicism, and love bundled up into that large body of his.

Her gaze dropped to his lips, fighting the desire to kiss him one last time.

Looking into his eyes again, she held his gaze.

I love you.

She *felt* it in the way he looked at her, though he didn't speak.

I love you too.

Olivia turned, and without looking back, left through the access door to join Gena.

Moments later, she thought she heard the soft ringing of harness bells in her inner ear as she descended the steps to the elevator.

Chapter Twenty-Five

Olivia shrugged out of her coat, exchanging it for the apron on the hook. Tying it around her waist, she washed her hands in the community kitchen's sink.

She'd spent the morning lounging on the sofa with Gena in her pajamas after a long hot shower, recounting everything that had happened.

After a hearty yawn, Gena had kissed her cheek and ordered her to nap before going to the shelter to help with the Christmas meals.

"What's on the menu tonight, Molly?"

"Funny, Liv. It's Christmas day."

Olivia turned, inhaling deeply of the warm turkey-filled aroma. "Of course. The place smells fabulous, Moll."

Molly grinned, "Thoughts on a tall, blond, bearded man?"

"Guilty. I'm so sorry I wasn't here all week to help you prepare everything."

"Oh, no worries. You know I love cooking." Molly waved a hand, then turned intent eyes on Olivia. "He was so sweet, when's your next date?"

"Never. He's gone home."

"Oh, sweety! I'm so sorry. No long-distance prospects?" Molly pulled Olivia into her ample embrace, making Olivia tear up. She sighed, voice soft. "I thought for sure he was perfect for you."

She sniffed, blinking away the unexpected tears. "He was. But not at this kind of distance." She rubbed the moisture from her eyes. "It's alright. We had a great time while it lasted. Besides, men just get me into trouble," she offered a watery wink.

Molly released her, rubbing her arms, expression sympathetic. "Well that's the truth, isn't it? Which reminds me, Mr. Anderson's daughter is here with her aunt. She wanted to talk to you."

Olivia's stomach tightened. "Best not keep her waiting then. Where are the desserts?"

Molly nodded toward the back room, "I'll grab the tray over."

Olivia moved toward the door, peeking out into the main room to locate Abigail Anderson. She found her in the back corner, slouched on a chair, arms folded, while the woman with her scrolled on her phone.

As Olivia turned to collect one of Molly's desserts, her gaze slid over an older man with a bad eye, making her breath stall.

Mr. Ayotte stared at her with his good eye, and noticing her attention on him, he smiled, lifting a grizzled hand in welcome.

Gosh, he looks so much like the temple guardian from Nick's past.

She smiled back, picking up an extra plate and moved toward his table. Placing the dessert dish next to his hand, she searched his face. "Happy Holidays, Mr. Ayotte. If you'll give me a moment, I just need to speak to someone."

"Of course," he smiled, picking up the spoon.

She patted his hand, drawing a deep breath before approaching Abigail Anderson. "Abby? You wanted to speak to me?"

The girl's head snapped up from her own phone. She swallowed, slipping it into her pocket. The woman next to her barely glanced at Olivia. "Ms. Boncoeur."

"Call me Olivia." She placed the dessert on the table and took the chair beside her.

Abby nodded. "Thanks." She picked up the spoon, poking at the frothy concoction.

After a long moment the woman next to her stood. "I'll be in the car."

Abby watched her leave before turning her gaze to Olivia. A tidal wave of emotion swept over her.

"I-I just wanted to thank you for not having my dad charged." Once she began, the rest was a rush. "I'm so sorry he attacked you. He's really not like that—it's just since he came back—he's been different and," she drew a deep breath. "I don't know. Different. And then the frustration of not finding work was too much—,"

Olivia's hand shot out, covering Abby's, calming her instantly. "I know. It's okay."

"Constable Greer's been coming around to check on me. He's been working to help dad get into a program for veterans."

"That's good. Graham's a good guy."

"I just—thanks. I love my aunt, but I don't want to live with her." Her eyes flicked toward the door.

Olivia nodded. "I'm so glad it seems to be working out okay. If you need anything, Abby, let me know."

"I will," Abby finally smiled, her shoulders relaxing. "I will."

Olivia tapped the table next to the dessert bowl as she stood. "Tell you what. You take that dessert with you, enjoy it, and return the dish some time next week. And if you're interested, Molly and I can show you the ropes around the kitchen." She tilted her head, drawing Abby's gaze toward Molly standing in the doorway bearing plates piled high with turkey.

"Yeah?"

Olivia nodded.

"Yeah, I'd like that." Abby beamed, getting to her feet. She threw her arms around Olivia. "Thank you so much."

"Happy Christmas. To you, and your dad."

Abby nodded, scooping up the dessert to take with her. "See you next week."

Olivia watched her go, then returned to Mr. Ayotte.

"Ms. Olivia." He licked the last of the whip cream from his spoon. "Tell Molly everything was perfect. How was your... vacation?"

As he held her gaze with his one good eye, something fell away, allowing Olivia to get a better read on him. She sensed his longevity and humming currents of power.

Then she knew. "Ayo? Nick's Ayo?"

The old man tapped the side of his nose, reminding her of when Nick had done that, their first night—first few moments together.

Olivia shivered. "You've been here, all this time? Does Nick know?"

"Oh, no. Not all this time. I come and go as needed. And it was time. For both of you."

"I don't understand."

"It's all in the timing." He nodded, giving his spoon another lick. "Any more of this back there?"

"You know there is." Olivia crossed her arms. "If you tell me what's going on."

Ayo turned his face toward Olivia, pinning her with his good eye.

She gasped when the milky eye swirled with opaline colour.

"Desserts are in the kitchen." Ayo said. "And your coat?"

Olivia eyed him with suspicion. Then finally nodded.

"Do you love him?"

Olivia stopped breathing.

Yes.

"I already know the answer to that. But enough to make sacrifices?" Ayo gave her a moment to collect her thoughts.

In a heartbeat.

She swallowed with a nod.

"I love this time of year. It always has the best desserts." The old man stood, reaching for his coat on unsteady legs. "Have you tried Dash's pie? Too bad he and Ms. Molly can't exchange recipes. They'd make bliss in a kitchen."

Numb, head reeling from the direction of the old man's questions, Olivia stood and led Mr. Ayotte into the kitchen.

"I knew you couldn't resist seconds, Mr. Ayotte." Molly winked, trading his empty bowl for another full one as Olivia took her coat off the hook.

"Thank you, Ms. Molly," Ayo beamed at the community kitchen's chef. "Through here is sufficient." He said to Olivia, waving a hand at the back door.

Molly watched with curiosity as Olivia helped Mr. Ayotte through the back door and down the snow-cleared steps into the alley.

They stood on a narrow path between high banks of snow pushed against the brick walls to either side.

Mr. Ayotte did some strange swirling of his hand as he muttered a few words and snapped his fingers, then grabbed the spoon and dug into the sweet dessert.

Olivia jumped as the alley lit up with a bright flash, followed by a pop.

Nick and Dolph appeared in the alley, each of them wearing an attached Nisse. Dolph's clung to the side of his blue head, Nick's hung off his thigh.

The impish Nisse faces grinned at Olivia before their attention swung to Ayo, sniffing.

"My goodness, this is tasty," he pointed the spoon at Olivia.

"What's this?" Nick demanded, attempting to dislodge the Nisse clinging to his leg. "Ayo? Liv?" His gaze dropped to the Nisse. "I didn't know they could do that."

"Their hands are full of maple syrup," Dolph groaned, wiping the Nisse's sticky hand from his eye.

Olivia studied him. He seemed lighter. A drastic change with the simple extraction of the tiny pebble of hate and grief and rage. Unable to help herself, she smiled up at him.

"Did I miss some?" his blue hands raked through his unkempt, recently washed hair.

"What this is, is a trade. Olivia for Dolph, if that is acceptable?" Ayo bent to place the bowl on the snowbank, immediately drawing the creatures from their perches. They dug into the dessert with both hands, shoveling cream and cake and other sweet bits into their mouths.

Nick glanced down at the sticky hand marks on his pants with a pained expression. Then straightened, finally leveling his gaze on Olivia's face.

It had only been a few hours since she'd left him on that rooftop, but her heart screamed that they'd been separated for an age.

"What's this trade you're talking about?" Dolph demanded, wiping his fingers on the crusty snowbank.

Ayo looked between the brothers. "Now that you're free of that infection, you may move on, if you wish." He held up a gnarled finger. "Not back to the mortal world. No, sorry, that time is past."

"Valhalla?" Dolph breathed.

Ayo shrugged. "Something like that. If you choose it."

"If I don't?"

"Back to the grove..."

"Or oblivion?" He swallowed.

"I only discuss the options mentioned. The rest is not my department."

Nick rolled his eyes. "You're as bad as the Council."

"Years of experience." Ayo nodded. "You've done well enough. I think that sort of work might be good for your Livvy here."

Olivia's heart pounded in her ears as she resisted the urge to reach for Nick's hand. To touch him once more, slide her fingers over his, reveling in their feel and warmth.

"How is that?" Nick and Olivia exchanged confused glances.

"Your young lady here is an anomaly, so to say," he nodded. "Death touched, djinn and dragon touched, with a deep Grove bond."

Olivia blinked.

Ayo waved a hand. "I've been instructed to relay that, with the Nisse's blessings, Olivia may stay for an extended period, such as the duration of winter. In the spring, she can return to her world, continue doing all the good deeds that could use her gentle touch. Then, you may reunite at the annual Council meeting. With her real-world experience, she'd be able to help 'guide things' in the right direction."

"And all the while, we continue our work in the groves. Stay the course." Nick's expression remained guarded as he looked from Olivia to Ayo.

Ayo tapped the side of his nose with a twinkle in his eye. "Your crew are content to continue on, knowing the Ascension is coming."

Olivia's head reeled, chest heaving as she stared at her boots, her breath puffing like a chugging steam engine.

"They'll try again? The Consortium?"

"Of course they will. And the grove must be protected."

"Olivia?"

"Gena—?"

"Cupid is harrying Vixen to develop a dedicated line for her."

Olivia turned to look at the closed kitchen door.

It's busy season, now.

"You've already enlisted Abigail Anderson to replace you. She'll do well, drawing in some of her friends to help out." Ayo said before she could utter the questions.

"I'm happy to go with Ayo; you can take my Nisse back with you," Dolph offered Olivia. "Besides, everyone's been lamenting your absence all day."

He drew a deep breath, turning to Nick with sad resignation in his eyes. "I'm sorry things weren't different between us. Brother."

Nick's throat worked beneath his beard. "Me too." He nodded, reaching out a hand to Dolph. "Me too."

Dolph accepted it. "See you in the next part of the afterlife, I suppose."

"Olivia?" Ayo drew her attention.

She turned tear filled eyes to the old man, sniffling, heart full of anguish from watching the estranged brothers. "Yes, Mr. Ayotte?"

The old man tipped his head toward Nick, who stared back at her with such intensity it took her breath away.

They stared at one another.

It was only supposed to be one night.

But she knew. Knew her heart would be safe with this man—if he chose to accept her.

She swallowed her rising hope.

His eyes flicked to Ayo with an imperceptible nod. "I'd be foolish not to accept such a perfect gift."

"On Christmas day," Ayo agreed.

Nick turned his dark eyes back to Olivia.

Snickering bounced off the frozen brick walls as two sets of little hands pushed the backs of Olivia's legs, sending her forward into Nick's arms.

In the circle of his arms, Olivia slipped hers around his back, murmuring. "Do you want me with you for months at a time?"

"I want you for eternity, Livvy." He whispered over her lips. "But I will accept what I can get."

She rose on tip toe to meet him, heart melting at the tenderness in his kiss.

"I love you," he said as he opened his eyes to hers.

Her fingers caressed his bearded cheek, stroking his lower lip. "I love you too, Nick."

Little voices cheered, sticky hands patting their legs with glee.

"Good, that's settled. The Nisse will be back for you in three days." Ayo said.

"Perfect." Olivia smiled, turning within Nick's arms to look at Mr. Ayotte. "I still have meals to serve."

Nick's hand slid under her coat, untied the knot of her apron and took a step back so that he could tie it around his waist. "Let's get to work then."

Ayo's laugh echoed around them as he clapped a hand on Dolph's shoulder, taking the somewhat redeemed Alfar with him when he disappeared.

The Nisse waved and were gone in a blink, leaving the two alone in the alley.

Snow drifted down, caught on the light breeze floating by the dull back door light.

Olivia looked up as the flakes clung to her face.

"Looks like we're in for a snowstorm tonight." Nick murmured.

"I have good boots on, and my place isn't far." Olivia grinned at him.

"Perfect." His gaze swept her face as he lowered his lips to hers once more. "Perfect."

~

If you enjoyed Gift, please consider leaving a rating or a review.

...For more Enchanted Ardor, read Gena's story in Wish!

~

Jolena Kane makes appearances in the GPSA: Aquatic Investigations and the Dragon Island series.

Dragon Island

Dragon Heat
Dragon Rogue
Dragon Blood

EveL Worlds : FUCN'A

Tough Nut
Diamond in the Ruff
Honeyed Nut
Gorilla in the Hiss
FUCN'A Collection One
Pedigree Collection

Global Paranormal
Security Agency

Awakened
Surfacing
Polestar
Aquatic Investigations
Prowler

Enchanted Ardor

Gift
Wish

Finely Aged

Dragon Steel

The Kindred Chronicles

Healer
Mercenary

The Nightshade Guild

Destined Time
Trial by Blood

The Soaring Dragon Chronicles

Return Flight
Changeling

Jodi Kendrick

Jodi Kendrick lives in Eastern Ontario Canada with her *Favourite Person* and chompy furbaby, while their adult children explore the wider world.

As a romance author, she writes in paranormal, fantasy, steampunk & gaslamp subgenres, and sometimes delves into urban fantasy and paranormal women's fiction. Her characters are often quirky, sometimes cranky, but they all woman-up and get the job done while their partners ensure they survive with all their bits and bobs attached.

A history enthusiast and word dabbler most of her life, she enjoys exploring 'beyond-the-everyday' and the 'time-before-now', discovering relationship threads weaving individuals through time and place. She's rarely seen without flashy notebooks and colourful pens.

Follow Jodi on Social Media: